FIELDS OF NEW YORK
European writers acquiring freedom

N McNally

FIELDS
of
NEW YORK

European writers acquiring freedom

N McNally

2nd Edition, 2023

ISBN 9783757887537

Published and Printed by BoD – Books on Demand, Norderstedt
Editor: N McNally
Layout & Typesetting: Boris Siebs

Me and you, 14 years of age.
Too bold and cool for school.
We got homies who do Hip-Hop.
One is on the two and twos,
one is spitting the lyrics,
another one is doing the dance
and all together we use the colour cans.

New Yorks largest export,
5 elements that give the youth a chance.
Juvenile energy flows free and a passion
is born within me.
In light and darkness, we trust,
the city is ours, courage grows I can't get bust.
Adventure, pleasure, adrenalin kicks.
It's not yet art, it's friendship,
me, you, I am Somebody.

My conscious is aware of a limitless horizon,
wheels of steel transport the feeling
of being real.
Graffiti was a foundation of cheekiness, difference
and confidence.

No fence was too high, no tunnel to deep,
we always succeed.
New York gave birth to what we live,
a Kingdom at the end of our tracks.
Definitely to be captured and conquered
to crown your personal fame.

INDEX

1

BACK IN THE DAYS YOU HAD TIME

Growing up in a Paris suburb, Fluor discovered quickly while travelling into the capital for his apprenticeship that lots was to be done. Passion, dedication and good friendship where his key elements on his created path to recognition.

The last year of the twentieth century was a beginning for billions of developments. Think or imagine anything you like. You've begun to read my book. Why did I begin to write? Have you something in mind that you would like to begin, start with? Then just do it. After a while you'll face a further decision, recalling and questioning your affection for the newly begun task. The rhythm of nature replicates it's self constantly, so taintless juvenile curiosity gave birth to this man's primal actions with colour markers. Growing up in a suburb of Paris, neighbourhoods were covered with tags and pieces which were then surrounded by other pub-lic scribblings, attracted the attention of this young man developing and living in the middle of it all.

Every boy and girl consciously or unconsciously looks out for an activity of a kind and eventually will find something of their own. You know yourself the various possibilities that have existed since man and woman began to scratch an itching body part to a human plunging itself towards the depths of a valley with a parachute that's supposed to open.

So, this young man found out for himself that his mind and senses occupied with forming a personal consciousness were being enlarged through graffiti.

The suburb was his playground and world, while Parisville still lay in a faraway distance and wasn't considered for extended outings yet.

Our lad gladly embraced the activity and attitude attached to graffiti and he titled himself Fluor. Seeing the different styles and tags in all their quantity, Fluor realized rapidly that, to him it was all about outdoing the existing graffiti. Find a better more exposed spot to paint and place an even bigger piece or tag there than the writer did before him. The activity on the streets suited him much more than the compulsion within the school system. Fluor's teachers and others responsible for him accepted his disbelief in school and he was sent, also in the year 1999, to Parisville to begin an apprenticeship. Fortunately for him there was a spray can store near his education training where he permitted himself to self-service. Well not quite, he bought one can and the other two cans were for free. Fluor's aim was to fill his daily traveling routes between suburb A, and B Paris with tags and pieces. This included his public transport lines, the motorways side walls and the streets of Paris leading to his apprentice school.

Unfortunately for Paris did the shopkeeper only notice Fluor's behaviour later than earlier, making Fluor run out the store onto the city's streets with the shopkeeper on his heels.

By now he was familiar with most of the paintable surfaces and was trying to combine quantity and quality to an equal balance. Like many another, Fluor had his close band of brothers and they valued their friendship highly, which was also put above Graffiti activities and still maintains itself till today. Within the subway painting scene, where Fluor will soon emerge into, social contacts are different and kept impersonal and are short lived.

In the meantime, Fluor remained active with a thriving appetite for more. His area of activity grew larger and more diverse across the French metropolis. The aim for a young man like him was to go *all city*. To conquer the town and the advertisement industry by out doing their gained publication surfaces, so that yourself, becomes more present than them in public space.

In technique that means to be visible on every metropolitan bus line, tram line, subway line wall and every suburb transit line adding on the motorway walls in and outside of town and last but totally not least your presence in every neighbourhood and town arrondissement.

Slightly comparable with ambitions of climbing a career ladder. Movement, passion and courage are vital and not to forget, discipline rewards the perpetrator. In 2003 and 2004 Fluor mostly went underground to fill the scarce vacant spots in the metro tunnels. During 2004 on one of his numerous painting walks through the Parisian metro tunnels he occasionally bumped into parked subway train compositions. At this time, he did not feel enabled to paint this new surface. Never the less he felt curious and yarned to expand his artistic endeavours. So, a one-minute piece, as described was set on a green and white metro wagon as a first experiment. Which left him and his friends realizing later on that night that a whole new world of possibilities lay ahead of them.

The atmosphere that hangs in the sticky and warm tunnel air, surrounding the prominent transportation object invaded the senses of these young men. The guys fell under the spell of this nerve tickling challenge and submitted themselves to the subway game. Fluor and his friends knew it was a different league and they felt ready and confident enough to take the city's transportation company with all their different employees on. There would follow an intense game of hide and seek and paint.

Pleasure overtook Fluor and he enjoyed his venturing into the semi dangerous activity. Along with all the other developments which over took his body and consciousness. Not everybody could do what he was doing, it was special, secret, hard core and reserved for the brave. He knew and felt its significance, but him and his friends realized that they were not alone in the tunnels. Numerous human tunnel rats were crawling through the same hatches and passageways of the Metro system below the parisienne boulevards like them. The *tags* and *pieces* left behind in the tunnels gave life to the unseen participants till now, who then slowly began to emerge into Fluor's newly discovered world. Tags accompanied by their executing figures where suddenly standing in front of him. He had only heard of these individuals through stories or seen their pseudonyms while travelling through Paris. Once he met a writer or writers as a crew, information relating to certain painting spots and places got requested, shared or was kept secret for self-benefit. The Paris Metro system is so big and challenging, everybody involved wanted to be as good as possible up to date with the various activities of the other crews. One could explore future possibilities by one's self, misrelying on anyone's help, which would give you respect and acknowledgement within the scene.

Fluor's attitude and intentions towards the scene were upright and positive. He kept on noticing more and more a kind of deceptive hypocrisy hidden behind the questions and actions of other writers. It wasn't his intention to conquer the (to him inexistent) rivalling competition, take what it may cost. To prove that he and his crew are the toughest, slickest and menace bunch of lads reaching out for the top position in the graffiti field. Which was, accompanied by admiration and respect for executed achievements. Experiencing new thoughts and feelings surrounding his life and the scene where changing his perspective, which eventually led to his substitution and abandonment of the in-official RATP game.

Two years past without Fluor engaging in any metro Graffiti related activities. Maybe the distance he looked for in the meantime from the graffiti activists did him good, because in the year 2007 Fluor and a friend made their comeback on the metro's of Paris.

It was the perfect time for Fluor's comeback because the whole metro painting scene of Paris was in full swing doing *whole cars, t2b's* and a quantity of *panels* on most of the underground lines. This continued for a couple of years till eventually in the year 2010 the RATP thought they had to take action against the on-going activities in their properties. Enough was enough and the RATP intended to regain the upper hand over the transport system and show who was actually in charge. Their internal security forces got expanded and the communication with the police department was intensified while technical sensors and surveillance got upgraded and shortly after the harvest began. Arrests were being made leaving many a writer worried if he would be the next to be paroled off to court. Fluor became anxious as well making him realise that the bold and cheeky days were probably going to decline and that their approach towards painting activities had to be seriously reconsidered. Painting missions now, where done once a month, accompanied with a more professional approach.

Fluor and his friends kept their game even tighter and more to themselves. Actions were planned well in advance and weren't getting pushed to full hardcore anymore and unnecessary risks were reduced in hope of more safety from prosecution.

Most of the time the missions went well, rarely did the guys have to flee from the spot and when they did have to run, the escape routes were clear from the beginning. They even used technical equipment and not everyone included in the action was there to paint. Some were there to provide security for the painters. This more professional approach to the game with its required handlings didn't mean the fun and pleasure got larger, it was rather the opposite. The addiction to metro painting stayed consistent, but the most important reasons for doing it were slowly withdrawing themselves from Fluor. He began to reflect what he actually was doing. Why was he functioning and operating more like a robot on the missions? Why was his passion dissolving and why was commitments grip letting go of him or him letting go of her? Was professionalism distinguishing his love for the game or was it rather life and it's mysterious paths that were attracting personal evolutionary thoughts in his mind. It's a stressful life when you're always in a state of alert, in fear of that door being knocked down any moment or just having to disappear in a shitty cell for a couple of weeks. The parisienne cops were doing detective work and the guys who had chosen an employment with the police, really fancy themselves and

14

enjoy the liberties accompanying the membership in that band of brothers. Bumpy knuckles. Abuse of their sovereign positions to disillusioning extents.

An invitation reached Fluor letting him know that he was warmly welcome to visit the city of New York. He had learnt rather late about NYC'S Hip-Hop history and wasn't too familiar with its virtues. Till now he had been living the NYC Hip-Hop lifestyle but the parisienne way. American music, movies, clothes styles made in the USA had brought him joy and got him interested. He was glad to book a flight allowing him to spend a month in NYC at the end of 2010.

Arriving in New York, he embraced the lights, the people, the buzz and straight away began to feel the weight of history as he rode through the tunnels and over the bridges of the New York City public transport system. Going along he noticed the importance of the subway too the cities citizens. A couple of days past by before his friend arrived from another north-eastern American city leaving him in the meantime to himself. He enjoyed the space his friend's absence gave him. In this short time, he had begun to feel at home.

His style of dwelling was similar to the European Interrail way when traveling, being able to use the apartment of his host who had recently left Paris for work in the city of New York. He camped out on the floor of the house without any fuss. You're having a great time all a long and it doesn't really lie in the nature of an Interrail writer to moan or groan about his sleeping situation. Three weeks were set aside to explore and see what New York had in hand for Fluor and his friend. The last week of their stay was going to get sacrificed for the challenge of putting their name up, up on the city's subway. The last week of his vacation arrived quicker than he had thought, and plans had to be made for that vital stage. In the meantime, Fluor and his friend had commuted all over the city in search of a suitable spot for their mission. It wasn't an easy choice for them when they saw the number of various layups and yards spread out over the entire city.

One afternoon as they were strolling along, looking and examining places of interest our two men bumped into a bunch of young writers, well that's what they called themselves. Like one does, Fluor and his mate spoke with the boys and Fluor mentioned the subject *yards* but these boys weren't keen on sharing any information about the certain, known to them. Never-the-less they wouldn't have to depend on them, because Flour was capable and willing to lead the two of them. The big yards up in the Bronx got ruled out due to the brutal barbed wire fences and the constant labour in and around the subway cars. Underground spots didn't get mentioned. Maybe Fluor and his mate didn't like the idea of being closed in that tight. In a writer's emergency situation, needing to flee the scene as quick as possible, tunnels don't provide many getaway options.

All along though, Fluor had kept one spot in mind since he had arrived in New York. It was an elevated layup on a bridge on the J line in north-east Brooklyn.

Arriving there, quietness had surrounded the spot and it looked cool to him. He knew other guys who had painted there before, so it should, he thought, work out fine to get their mission done here.

A couple of days before Fluor and his friend had set out for their action had they met some old school Yankee writers and among them, was the living legend SEEN. A well-known figure to most writers all over the world. He stared himself in the famous Hip-Hop movie STYLE WARS. You could see him engaged with his passion, Graffiti, on the NYC subway back in the eighties. Till today he has stayed faithful with his tools and passion, involving himself in the Art world. When Fluor and his mate had told SEEN what their secondary intentions were in New York, he laughed at them and couldn't really understand their goal.

"Hey man, those days are long passed. I was up like many others, as you hopefully know. Today you ain't even going to see you're piece running, so what's the point. And these subways nowadays aren't even American. Today's cars are Asian made, the real New York American made subway wagons are becoming artificial reefs in the sea just off Coney Island. Man, this is toy shit, but if you want, I can give you KRYLON cans from back in days. They'll give you an impression of how we did our pieces."

Fluor and his mate found his proposal to cool to reject and gladly accepted his offer.

The clock was advancing towards midnight as the two men left their dwellings with their old spray cans. Only a few people were sharing the subway with them as they made their way through New York to the chosen spot. Some people had their gins lowered on their chests, others were reading pocket books. Whilst the general person was stroking or touching his mobile phone. Fluor and his friend were sitting next to each other, backpacks between their legs and their thoughts devoted to the upcoming mission. Peace and quietness filled the otherwise rattling subway wagon as it rolled up the stations on its way towards the end of the line. Every now and then Fluor and his mate gently broke the quietness to exchange some details about their mission. Both their faces expressed determination and their nerves were relatively calm. Their intentions were to carry out their piece if the situation allowed it, then there would be no reason for them to turn on their heels. The subway arrived at the station where the parked train composition of desire lay waiting for them. It stood just a couple of hundred meters beyond the stations platforms. The men weren't going to approach yet, because they had planned to pass the object of desire twice by subway to get a first glance of the spot for anything sus pious (peculiarities). Back they rode, and all looked well. Now was the time for them to leave the station, imitating tired workers. As they walked down the stairs of the station and out into the surrounding neighbourhood, one could think they were home-goers. The surroundings below their parked composition had to be looked at for suspious goings-on, such as cop alike people sitting in cop alike cars or dudes in pairs, pretending to be chill'in on the block. After getting an oversight, our painters conclusion of things were going their way. Now back in the deserted station, the two were able to descend down the platforms steps and run carefully, making as least a noise as possible, towards the gently shimmering silver colossus. Reaching the nose of the subway train they slowed their pace and came to a stop between two carriages. With caution they climbed up over the hanging cables and chains connecting the two carriages and excited by what they were doing, entered the wagon in a merry state. Once inside, the view out through the windows was overwhelming. Below them lay the dimed streets and as far as they could see twinkling golden lights were all around them. Standing in that dark wagon, gazing outwards, made Fluor feel like himself was in STYLE WARS and what he saw was truly the US and A and he was assured that he would accomplish the mission.

Patience was still required from both of them as they sat down in the wagon to wait for the operating subway to pass. Afterwards they would have vacant tracks for approximately twenty minutes. The subway train, the one they intended to paint, which was also the one they were sitting in, was set between two tracks on which the night service operated. Till now nothing strange or suspious had occurred to Fluor and his friend during their observations and safety checks. At last it was time to place the caps on to the KRYLON cans. Fluor chose to paint his piece with fat caps. These caps withdraw the colour from the cans under an intensified pressure. This widens the colour line more than other caps do. Two colours were set for the fill-in of his five-letter piece. Another colour was for the background of the piece and to his serious distaste he only had black for his out-lines. Normally he wouldn't use black because he prefers colour out-lines. And to give his piece that essential gleam or shine, white was waiting to get used as well. A gentle screech pierced the night's quietness as the upcoming subway train came to a halt in the nearby station, bringing both men to their feet.

As soon as the subway train had passed, the lads will exit the wagon the same way as they had entered, meaning those dodgy cables and chains will slightly be in there way again. Here she comes, and the wagon filled itself with light from the passing subway train. Out the door they went, probably not to return to the inside of a cosy sleeping New York subway train again. Over the cables and chains, they climbed down onto the tracks. The two-looked left and then right to ensure that everything was really okay. Feeling comfortable they withdrew their KRYLON cans in front of the painting spot. Fluor pushed down the cap on his can and a thin jet of colour emerged from it, but only for a couple of seconds. To his dismay, the colour now, was squirting out from beneath the cap and not through it. This meant his spray can was having an overkill and it required a cap that withdrew the colour with less pressure. A sort of agony overcame Fluor as he was forced to change all the caps on his cans. Never-the-less he had to continue and get over the disappointment as quick as possible. Time was running, and the next subway was down the line on its way to them.

The caps were replaced with skinny ones which release the colour with less pressure. Fluor tried to accelerate his painting speed to catch up the lost minutes, but those KRYLON cans wouldn't let him achieve it. The cans were slow, the colour was dribbling down the surface and the whole situation began to make Fluor's nerves bubble. "Fuck!" thought Fluor as he realised that the remaining time wouldn't be enough for him to finish his piece, so he decided to expel one letter out of his name. After that decision he finally was able to concentrate better on what he was doing. The action wasn't going exactly how he had imagined it too go. Whilst painting he looked at his flanks, where he saw his mate working away on the subway. The scenery and atmosphere around them made it worthwhile.

Fluor finished his piece, stood back, looked at it and nodded to himself. Better than nothing he thought. His friend needed a couple of minutes longer to finish, so Fluor tagged the names of friends around his piece to greet and acknowledge them.

Although everything was going fine, Fluor's instinct was pushing him to leave the place. Come on, things had to go a bit quicker, because the operating subway was due to arrive. Two flashes rapidly lit up the surrounding darkness and their colour work was instantly visible and captured on camera. A last look back at the spot and their production before their minds set their legs into running mode. Through the night's fresh air, back towards the stations platform the two men ran where they arrived, just in time to throw away their cans and mount the operating subway train. On entering the warm carriage, the two sat down. The palms of their hands met each other in mid-air as they clapped too seal the accomplishment. Drinks in the form of ARIZONA Ice Tea followed as they waited in a lively bar for dawn to come and lighten up their panels. At day break the two went back to the place of their acquired freedom. Suddenly a great idea sprung into Fluor's mind while they were standing beneath their painting spot. The main door of the building opposite their pieces was surely possible to open with a credit card. From there they would be able to take pictures from the houses roof. Rooftop doors in New York are always accessible and open most of the time. As easy as it sounds, so easy was it done. The two were up on the roof where they had a wonderful 360° degrees view of the urban scenery. The background in daylight suited their colourful pieces sitting there on the shiny silver subway train perfectly. This was the kind of scenery Fluor liked their pieces embedded in. An honest backdrop like this residential surrounding. He didn't like places artificially touched by the hungry progressive people who were trying to widen the gap of realities. City scenery with symbolic monuments or famous artefacts in the background didn't touch him and could turn the result of the action into a holiday postcard.

What the two men saw didn't disappoint them. Their names were clearly leadable and thinking what had happened to Fluor's cans, it was excusable. On the other hand, it was still the New York City subway with their pieces on it. Their passion chill'in there in Januarys morning sun light. Pride swelled up in both of the men's chests as they took their remembrance and proof photos at their leisure. Tired and a bit warn down from the night's activity, the two lads feeling content, set off home for some hours of sleep.

Later on, Fluor and his mate met up with their other friend living in New York and together they met some dinosaurs of New York graffiti. "Yeah man we did it, everything went fine except for that moment when my colours went squirting all over the place."

"Where and which line did you paint?" asked one of the old schoolers. "The J line," they replied. "Sorry guys don't want to disappoint you but that ain't the proper subway. Did no one ever tell you that the numbered lines are the real deal!"

"Fuck it" sprung immediately in to Fluor's mind as he listened with despair to this fellow speaking. When he heard this his pride was hurt and his feelings went from elation to desolation. Two days of anxiety, work and energy, to be told afterwards, it ain't the real thing. Fuck, this shit it ain't over yet, Fluor thought as he met his friend's eye and expression. Looking at each other both exactly knew what had to be done. Straight afterwards, further yards containing the seemingly real subway trains got inspected and checked out. Unfortunately, luck wasn't on their side at any location of interest. There was no realistic opportunity to be found for a fresh action for them. A couple of nights sleep settled the most of their disappointment and their hopes of achieving the predicted goal was postponed to another time and visit.

To lender their soft aching hearts, Fluor and his mate accepted a final invitation. Meaning they were led by the hand to a further action up the east coast in a city that was equipped with an underground system before they left for the old continent. Sitting on the plane among all the different passengers, Fluor's thoughts were of a warm and grateful nature. The New York City subway won't be his biggest achievement in the painting game, but maybe his future visits to New York will change his mind or he'll set himself totally different goals that have a larger purpose and meaning to his life.

And don't forget that there is possibly no wrong time to give that newly found interest it's worthwhile beginning.

2

THE GHOST YARD

Having seen the Graffiti documentation movie
STYLE WARS on National television in 1983, Balwin out
of Germanys Rheinland,wanted to be part of the letter
writing element. Being close to Graffiti's springtime,
New York city called out for Balwin to come and see for
himself.

Sheets of white paper filled with colourful sketches are
scattered upon the low living room table set in front of the
sofa with Balwin sitting upon it practicing his styles. Si-
multaneously but unnoticed by him because of his deep
occupancy a remarkable evening sky is drawing itself,
viewable through the square glassed holes in the wall, together on the horizon above New York City's boroughs
pulling the days last light out through the room's windows
leaving space for the advancing darkness to spread out inside the room. If Balwin would lower his pencil for a second and guide his eyes away from the sheet of paper in
front of him and follow the retreating rays of light out the

window would he be able to join other admirers watching pumpkin orientated colours in the sky being mixed and exchanged by the minute with intense and darker tones until nature settled once again for its eternal night colour. Emerging out of the kitchen comes Why-U's voice startling concentrated Balwin who realises instantly that it's too dark for drawing. "What did you say?" replies Balwin as he gets up to switch on the light. "Seeing you so absorbed with your styles, has me wondering if you've got your letters wright for this evening," asks Why-U who was in the kitchen sowing up a hole on the front side of a coat of his. "Yeah man with light in the room I think I know which styles I'll use tonight and it's alright for me to do a whole car ay Why-U? I really want to get that burner done tonight. I hope things will go our way and bless us all the way," he continued. "Don't worry big boy, as long as no rain comes the New York way, we'll be rule'n that yard tonight. Everything you need to get your whole car done is available inside the yard. You just get yourself ready for tonight's performance and our intrude into one of the worlds's greatest subway yards you'll ever get to see and be able to experience," Why-U confidently convinced him.

Why-U was now standing in the door frame wearing his fixed down coat and grinning at Balwin. The expression on his face was suggesting that the night's excursion was probably going to be better than anything Balwin had experienced before. Noticing Why-U's comfortable mimic, Balwin's thoughts already slipped off into the yard with him getting his dream done in a style and fashion close to the glory days of New York's graffiti. He could remember Tierra another New York writer and friend of his talking about the time when all the subway trains of New York were full of Graffiti. Carriages covered from top to bottom with high quality pieces, called *burners*, were running in traffic. Till the Mayor of the city in 1982 had enough of the crime attracting art, as they say, and came up with the idea of giving the carriages a fresh coating to clean the situation up. His idea got realised and seven thousand subway carriages came out of the maintenance centres repainted in white winning the project the nickname "the great white fleet" referring to the white fleet in Detroit after racial unrests.

Imagine being a writer then in that moment. One must have had a two-sided sense. On the one hand the drag of loss and extinguish (expire) but also the feeling of gratitude underlined with instant eagerness to get going on their freshly repainted work surfaces. A clean start again. Round two for all the various actors involved in the game.

History

Growing up in Germanys North-Rheinland region in the upcoming hip-hop era, Balwin first made contact with the culture in 1984 through his participation with the element Breakdance.

One out of five elements defining Hip-Hop. He is between the age of twelve and fourteen and fitted with a genuine amount of testable independence granted to him by his parents.

Breakdance is a vibrant and physical skilful engagement with music which requires a strong alertness to one's coordination of the singular body part movements accompanying the rhythm and bass beat of a Hip-Hop music track. Breakdance like any other dance style needs a lot of intense practice and dedication. When able to master a whole figure connected with the wright footwork like the turtle or the bridge you can compete your moves with other dancers and join a battle ceremony held mainly between two or several crews. The crew whose individual dancers, who can also compete in pairs or form a bigger unit of participants to produce a string of moves, impress the onlookers the most shown through loud cheering with their all-round style and ability win the battle. Beside this new developing element of Hip Hop in his region Balwin became aware of a further element popping up on buildings and trains.

Through the screening of the semi-documentary movie STYLE WARS followed by other films like WILD STYLE and BEAT STREET on national television and in nationwide cinemas in 1983 many German youths were directly confronted with this new culture form emerging out of poor neighbourhoods in New York. A flare of excitement and adventure circulated throughout the film creating in many a young man and possible also in women a curiosity for its art. On Balwin's way to school or in train station buildings he would frequent and use as a playground after school with friends to mess about and exchange news and one's mysteries of growing up he independently noticed tags and pieces coming into existence around him.

Their existence appeared to him as rather strange and when standing in front of a wall piece he hardly was able to decipher its letters. Seldom pieces were already running on the regional trains like the ones in that particular movie STYLE WARS and it seemed to him that many of the boys he spent time with were tagging and involving themselves in such actions as well. Inspired and interested by what he saw he decided independently to create and engage on his own behalf designing a load of small stickers containing his tag name. He stuck them up in and around his school. Following shortly afterwards came his primary will to execute a Graffiti piece so his first encounter with spray cans took place. Once darkness had spread and offered anonymity he set out with a can and drew his Outlines upon a wall of his school. Seeing the first part of his effort finished he went home intending to return the following night to do the pieces fill-in and complete the Graffiti which he briskly did.

It is the year 1986 and Hip-Hop culture here in the North-Rheinland has firmly wiggled its roots into human life through the actions and dedication of its growing number of participants. Close by, a couple of hours travel by train or car lay the harbour city of Amsterdam which had developed till now the most active and vibrant community of Hip-Hop culture with a notable influence into many other communities across Europe. The city's walls and Subway carriages gained an immense use and were obliged to hold the out numerous names of writers participating across the town. The Hip-Hop community in the town objectively undeniable received naturally awareness and attention from its visitors which was commendably passed on in the developing scenes in the surrounding towns and cities. So, one day Balwin was taken along by his parents for a holiday to this famous to him City.

Once in Amsterdam the young tall and slender growing boy who is now about fifteen years old seeing the all-round extent of his equal occupancy was eager to engage himself with local writers and cooperate. Being a writer, your outer appearance could be estimated by another writer due to your choice of style and the colour spots sticking upon you. Having found a can store or brought some along on the trip Balwin set out looking for a place in town where he most likely would meet his equivalents. Coming across a Hall of Fame he set himself up creating a piece. He wasn't alone on the wall and shortly afterwards inquiries got exchanged among the young men present. Passing time together the locals put forward an invitation to Balwin if he desired to join them on a Metro painting action in the next days. This being his first opportunity to paint upon a train which he certainly had given thoughts too in the meanwhile eagerly and happily accepted their friendly invitation.

Arriving at the meeting point spot on time Balwin was greeted by six local painters and they set off to the Metro yard in the brightness of the day. Once there outside the Metro yard the only obstruction standing between the group of lads and the Metro carriages was a one meter in height fence which obviously wasn't going to stop seven agile young men from hopping over it. Having easily entered the yard with no one to stop them in broad daylight all went about his task on the shiny silver steeled channelled surface. Balwin had enough cans to divide its colour up for three small pieces. While one fellow who wasn't in the best condition for painting had one arm in a plastered caste never the less still did a scrappy filled up whole car from one end to the other and from bottom to top. Another chap lay on the roof of a carriage overlooking the scene with the rest of the group doing their pieces hoping that the paint wouldn't run out because this was the only case that was going to stop them. While one who had his headphones on listening to music wondered about the yard leaning here and there against the carriages or the fence keeping an eye out for them. What a nice circle this was to fulfil ones first piece on a train precise a Metro train and it certainly created hunger for more of the sort.

The primary experience must have left him fairly impressed because it led him to further activities and engagement with him subsequently sustaining his will to continue his new approved activity. The effect a Graffiti piece provided upon the side of an operating train amused him and convincing determined it as his main goal of contribution.

The year 1986 was his beginning to a commitment intensely maintained by him all along his path through teenager-hood venturing into the age of adult-hood. Back home in his city Balwin shared his painting experience with his friends and they came up with the aim to explore further cities in Germany and those of the surrounding countries. One wasn't too sure about painting one's own train system and the way things where set up around it. Possibilities didn't seem to be available. Liberty and the boundless approach that evolved inside oneself as soon as your back was turned upon your domain area didn't exist yet locally.

You could relax and feel safer once off your home turf in the distance and unknown. A jolly outing is always a terrific adventure, so train tickets got organized and off they went to Frankfurt, Hamburg and Munich to orchestrate their painting actions. A nice thing for a kid around fifth-teen years of age and on top not really difficult to achieve except if you're a shy and cautious weak kid but also then courage to friendship can channel to new waters. Balwin now around the age of seventeen was willing to explore further. Plans were created to venture abroad so the Interrail ticket came in hand to manage such prolonging's. England, Holland, Skandinavia, Switzerland where all accessible with just one purchased train ticket.

Kept close by through his travelling and the constant confrontation with his cherished task remained the question about the origin of it all. Balwin was aware of his affection for the skills and styles embedded in Hip-Hop that he had once embraced when transferred to Europe from North America and came to the conclusion that the heritage site was worth a prior visit possible to achieve.

Entering the year 1989 a lot had been seen and undertaken painting wise away from home and when seeing regional train after regional train sweeping into town belayed with colourful pieces his and his friend's realization towards their local surroundings was renewed and they put themselves together to overlook their terrain from an updated point of view. Now with their developed knowledge accurate for the mastering of the various train rest spaces around and in town a wave of train Graffiti began to swell throughout the North-Rheinland region and it spread and splashed itself covering train upon train leading to a circulation system redecorated vastly. The wave rolled and rolled throughout the nineties on a strong current wonderfully visible on the train fleet supported by the lack of blockers called specifically *the Buff*. Coming the end of the decade, it slowly but gradually smoothed out to single appearances one reason being the fusion of the North-Rheinland regional train system with other bordering regions enlarging the fleet of trains and cleaning stations.

Looking back to the mid-eighties when the first pieces popped up and you were able to sit inside the train enjoying the observation of the passengers response to your piece sticking on the outside and no one considered you could well be the artist behind it as you disembarked the train with your cans rattling aloud in your backpack with every step you took dressed affine to the culture. The pieces ran for days and weeks and only slowly rose the retaliation against their presence, which made the pieces endurance till today last only a couple of runs till a day or two.

In the meantime, though New York City still shun alight and Balwin's desire to attend its offering was met first in 1990. He proposed the insist to himself and his outcome was that the fountain of his culture form had to be experienced in New York which would close his circle of practice placing him and his contribution in a central position defined alone by him. The stories he had been told about the painting life in New York City where sweet music in his ears and every time an attached thought arose within him, it unleashed an eagerness to participate among the Appeltonions and achieve goals true to the originals of the game.

His intentions were to widen the first achievements done by a North-Rheinland local in New York and extend the brave and solid efforts already done by him in order to maintain the role of the successor familiar to participants of Graffiti in the North-Rheinland. Important to Balwin was also the development of a distinguishable and unique kind of style of his own which ended for him in a personalized and particular calligraphy. Just perfect for executions of his taste upon his keen suburban target. His styles where distinct and well recognisable.

Having received the contact dates of Yankee writers from his North-Rheinland comrade made Balwin ready to venture into the heartland of progress and prosperity. Contacts are essential to the individual on any trip to anywhere in the world if he or her is looking for upgrades, enrichments and prosperous developments in the fields of his or her interests. There is always more to gain and win due to the law of sharing.

Balwin arrived in New York for the first time in 1990 and kept returning annually for seven years. Each visit consisted a length of up to two weeks till a whole month. Sitting in the aeroplane with sometimes up to sixty cans in his baggage stored below deck he would generally wonder what kind of craziness would happen this time. His main dwelling in town was in a squatted house in the back then badly run-down South Bronx with not many people out of his hemisphere but after a couple of days in the neighbourhood people would greet him like their own due to his genuine stroll and his relationship with his Latino resident hosts.

Entering the new millennium his visits faded out and he found himself back in town twice but was left disappointed by the change in the surroundings besides feeling happy for the squatters whose house had gradually been legalized and put in to a good living condition. Never the less painting remained on his agenda but reduced to a minor extent subsequently practised in a moderate and adjusted manner, abstracted to the contemporary ways. Visiting this world-famous city time after time including his awareness to lengthen the spell of his stay to a span valuable for more content must have left him each time with tickled senses on meta levels seldom experienced by humans of this epoch.

Arriving in a city where one tells you or at least one did tell you in a distant time ago that, yes this is the city of dreams and all your imaginations can be realised if you attach yourself to, what? To the right temperature of a breeze and go-ahead pursuit it or follow your nose till you have gained the delighting answers and mimics you need for your intentions.

Rise from washing dishes to using a private mobility network taking you in mid-air across the Hudson River from A to B with the door opening key made out of valuable nature turned into paper with numbers in its corners or digital numbers printable by privates, which shortly afterwards could show its deceitful side of its otherwise discussable purpose. Surely if you're mental state is fostered with methods purposed or not to secure and stabilize your confidence and solid beneath you lays a domestic atmosphere infiltrated with egocentric ambition plus a non-existing glimpse of equality towards others, yeah then the sky is the limit and if your goal is succeeded here you're capable of repeating your intentions anywhere. But of course, there is more to it and looking above yourself, the sky ain't the limit is it?

Luckily for Balwin and many others similar to him, one might not have had financially the same settings, but when once aware of the mental importance in steel orientated Graffiti, the game is played on equal grounds and illegal or legal doesn't concern anymore. Everything is possible. If realised that the work you invest is accountable to you and the actual piece upon something special is your sizeable result, you get rewarded with respect and admiration. Aesthetics, skill and quantity intensify one's reward. New York City back in the 60's and 70's with all its thriving facets and different aiming directions gave Graffiti a crack for itself to squeeze and spread out all over the city and beyond bringing colour to various surfaces surrounding the city human. Till one day forces stern and dosh (money) orientated began to introduce renovation to the city. Public space got diminished, activities upon them confronted and narrowed by police presence combined with fixing up and regulating the majority of instable and exploitable surfaces valuable for business and profit.

But before those city developments Balwin was helter-skeltering across the city meeting his expectations, feeling whole and was always in close contact with the inhabitant that never sleeps. New York back then and beyond had a relaxed attitude towards Graffiti flanked by a *Vandal Squad* that wasn't as established and sternly engaged like today. Their involvement was of a lazy slow nature. The North-Rheinland surely didn't provide life on scales so vibrant as in New York and especially during its 70's, 80's and 90's. Humans venturing into those various cracks available back then where acquiring actions and feelings depending on a sense of freedom. Actions that no longer would bear the narrow-minded expectations of the majority of society living and increasing under the siege of capitalism.

Back in the Livingroom
The sketches that Balwin favoured the most out of all the ones he had just done during the fall of dusk where separated from the non-required ones and put to one side of the living-room sofa table. His idea was defined and transferred onto paper which left him content, happy and eager to begin the challenge of transferring it further, further across the city, further through the darkness of a yard, through anxiety and surprises till in the end he would be standing in front of the shiny surface of a Ney York city subway carriage where its final transformation could get completed.

The evening's preparations were underway and both Why-U and Balwin were now sorting the colours of their cans. Each piece that was going to get done tonight needed an individual prearrange and separate arrangement of its colours. Observing the number of cans spread out on the living room floor, the two hunched over them choosing and matching the colours in their imagination till placed next to the prearranged ones, signalled that something of an extended dimension was going to get pursued tonight. Music from Kool G Rap accompanied them filling the room with additional atmosphere. After twenty minutes they had the cans sorted and Balwin had around thirty of them to fulfil his ambitious goal. Both were in good spirit and in a confident state of departure. Their bags were packed, the shoestrings firmly tightened, trousers adjusted and buckled so Why-U suggested to make the move. Friends of Why-U were going to pick them up outside the building. Outside both men seated themselves each on one of the two side walls of the short flight of stairs leading up to the main entrance of the building, maintaining their exchange of words. Balwin mastered the English language pretty well so far and day by day constantly made improvements either in the pronouncement of words out of his vocabulary or by enlarging it. Admirable was his development in speaking the cities dialect which won him the most credits when he talked. He listened well and sporadically tried to make the imitation perfect of how the yank moves his jaws and turns and twirls his tongue while he drops his voice to a deeper tone when explaining or just talking. One definitely couldn't have said straight away to him after hearing him speak: your German aren't you! The numerous visits to big apple were letting his English ripen as well as his character. Merging towards age was an easy going, tolerant and respectful young man who was a happy chap to meet and greet humans living their lives on common grounds.

Few people were out and about at the time the two writers where waiting and most that passed by them popped into the corner store a stone's throw down the street. Some were noticeable branded by their previous or current drug lust viewable through their hasty movements and weathered faces.

But somehow, when hearing them speak in front of the corner store to whoever was there, their voices resembled positivity and hope in a resistant and hard-bitten holistic figure. Observing the passing figures while they're still waiting, Balwin told Why-U that he was slightly disappointed with himself for missing most of the tunnel's scriptures on their walk-through tunnels leading to a central park layup the other night. Balwin: "I was so focused on keeping a secure overview of our situation that I forgot to inspect the Tags on the walls closer. There must have been

twenty years of New York Graffiti spread out all along."
Why-U: "Sure homie, the place where we were the other
night served New York's writers as long as you just said.
Everybody who had the guts went Central Park subterra-
nean and left their markings on their way. Don't you do
the same when the situation is at ease and your surrounded by inviting surfaces?" Balwin: "Yeah bro, sure do if I've
got any colours left. But seeing and painting those old red
subways down there really equalises everything. Aren't
they going to get dumped soon or of course replaced?"
Why-U: "You were lucky player, they are seldom and are
already rare in existence due to their replacement." A car
with blaring hip-hop music is advancing down the street
light lit road towards them with a guy waving at them out
of the back window.

Pulling up at the sidewalk Balwin and Why-U pick
up their bags and approached their visibly merry friends in
the car. "All good brothers, ready to get pop'in," comes
questioning out of the car. Both underline their willingness
with optimistic and heartful hand clapping while greeting
each other. The bags get placed in the booth and the two
mount the ride, sharing the last vacant space in the back.
The car indicates and moves slowly out into the street.
Why-U still hasn't told Balwin where they are going so
Balwin puts the question to the creators of the cosily set in
group. The guy sitting in the front passenger seat, who is
Tierra answers first saying: "A spooky place way Uptown
which has gained its name, *Ghost Yard,* from certain stories and rumours. In the seventies 400 bodies got exhumed
from the then existing memorial ground leaving nowadays
sights of white figures floating around the buildings and
noses of the subway compositions parked on the premises.
But maybe they come from the salt workers who seemingly moved around covered in salt dust in the previous Salt

38

depot which was located somewhere there or around the place." "And there's another story," starts Luis who is sitting between the squashed bunch in the back, "of once heard piercing female screams on the brink of death cutting the nights silence emerging from a shed located in some down trodden dim lit area of the yard." Why-U continues mentioning the story of a writer who had been beaten to death by yard workers and afterwards was laid to rest beneath the yard's subway train tracks.

Sitting squashed between the four of them on the broad back seat, Balwin listened amused but couldn't help the irritating impulses arise in his conscious and thoughts. Instantly engaging his circling thoughts arose counter impulses which restored normality and tranquillity to his previsualized image of the described place.

For him the subway compositions should be standing neatly set in file, gleaming under the high-pitched lights and inefficiently secured like aged vintage uranium mines across the north of the countries states without hovering figures and there hunting ghost busters.

Balwin favoured his secondary thoughts, kept though close at mind his well-preserved ambition to survive any ill change in their ongoing situation. Asking more so as a joke Balwin wondered if they were going in strapped or at least with some specific protection and retreat plan. Tierra replied chuckling in his front seat that the river flowing past and beneath the Ghost Yard carried all sorts of noises from its embankment surroundings which results in undefinable echoes in the night air. Stick to one of us and you'll be fine.

Balwin poked Why-U who was sitting next to him in the ribs and thanked them all that he was allowed to proceed with them connoisseurs.

The car with the boy's chill'n to the easing sounds of Montell Jordan sped northwards amid reduced traffic heading for Broadway which descends from where they were going. The ride took about thirty minutes till they reached the junction leading off Broadway and into 207 street which marks the beginning of the Ghost Yard. They were now at the upper end of Manhattan Island close to where the Hudson river makes way for the Harlem river to flow down the east side of the island. Down 207 street they drove surrounded more or less by housing blocks verifying in size but not in colour because they were all out of brown bricks. Scattered between the housing units were general stores and shops a neighbourhood requires for its American daily bases. Reaching the end or the beginning of 207 street they turned into 10 Avenue where you could see beyond its pavement the buildings and flood lights belonging to the famous Ghost Yard. They continued up the street passing the whole length of the yard till they reached 215 street. The part of Tenth Avenue set parallel to the yard was covered by elevated tracks operated by the line number one.

Why-U told the driver to drive down 215 street, so they could quickly take a glance at the back entrance of the premises. Opposite the entry on the other side of the street and parked all along both sides of the street where vehicles from the city's garbage department. Arriving at the appointed place, they stopped with their view going straight out onto the dark and slow Harlem River.

Its flow also formed a natural boundary on one of the yards sides. But out there didn't lie their interest and all heads turned to look out the right side of the car.

Standing in front of them behind the back-entrance fence, reflecting brightly underneath the yards floodlights a short distance away were the lads declared target for that night. About twelve subway compositions were visible from their angle and after a short while they all agreed that no employee had been seen from neither of them. What they were looking at is officially called the 207-STREET RE-PAIR SHOP which consists of two maintenance facilities and serves the subway lines 1,2,3,5 and the A line. Here was the back entrance but only for official use. The writer's entrance was right on the opposite side of the grounds, so they reversed the car and headed back to 207 street.

The night's sky was covered with bright metropole clouds and the temperature close to midnight was thanks to the time of year in an enjoyable state. The lads got out of the car, glanced around for any suspious occurrences close by in their side street or in the distance down the road in the direction of the yard. Some of them stretched themselves loosening their joints from the snug car ride while the others took the bags out of the booth and off they went towards their entrance. "What a lovely wall, it's perfect to keep stray dogs out," said Balwin as he saw the height of the yards man made boundary. Something around two meters measured Balwin's eye. Each of them picked up something lying around that one could use to stand on so one was able to observe the other side of the wall standing at ease. A nice scene resulted itself out of their positions because their bodies were cut off by the shade produced by the wall, leaving six different shaped heads visible upon it. Eight additional subway train compositions could be seen from where they were standing and were pointed out as the definite and final painting targets.

The lads remained in position for about twenty minutes scarcely uttering a word to one another. Their eyes scanned every dark and bright space set between the trains and maintenance buildings till far across the yard over to the fence overlooking the river in search of movement and activity from the yard's employees. The only response they received during their observation was a faint mechanical noise emerging out of one of the facilities buildings on the other side of the yard accompanied by screeches from over flying seagulls.

Tierra signalled to the group to dismount their stools and they put their heads together to discuss their procedures. The trains they want to paint lie roughly 300 meters away from them.

No movements had been seen on the whole terrain and the erupting noise didn't really occur to them because it was well off in a distance and had been like that on previous visits without anything dissolving out of it. The path to their target was agreed upon and Why-U said he would take the lead. Why-U easily climbed the wall, dropped to the ground and withdrew all the bags.

One after the other followed. Crouching at the foot of the wall all took a final oversight of the ground. Spread out in front of them across the whole complex were loads of laid train tracks, over lighted by a handful of steel floodlight pillars raging into the nights sky and set between them sheds, singular wagons, piles of wood for the tracks with rubbish scattered among high grown weeds and other plants and of course the main reason for their presence, the numerous shining subway train compositions. Why-U made a hand gesture to follow, moved forward in a ducked position and the others singled in behind him. The group advanced quick and steady in their crouched positions with Why-U sticking to the most direct and more or less shaded path. Having reached the noses of the subway compositions they slipped into the passage set between the second and third composition. The lads straightened themselves knowing that the only way they could be seen now was from either end of the passage they were standing in. Balwin made a few steps with both arms stretched out with his fingers gliding along on the carriages steel surface while the others crouched again to handle the content of their bags. Tierra removed himself from the group but returned quickly with a broken chair in one hand and holding in the other one an empty oil barrel. Balwin was happy with the visibility conditions and seeing Tierra bringing those objects around the corner even more assured that he could proceed with his one-man whole car. Carrying the barrel Tierra came over to Balwin and told him where he was to paint and that the barrel was his. Just before he picked up his bag of paint and made his move to his painting place he suggested to Balwin that he should take his time. Well what could that mean thought Balwin as he attached the caps to his cans without making any further inquiries. Balwin was ready to get started. He looked to his left side to ensure himself that the others were also ready or if they had already started. Two of the group were set on the following carriage after his one and the other three were going to do carriages opposite (next) their compositions. Pleasured by what he saw while looking down the passage, Balwin pushed down his cap guiding the emerging colour to the lines he wanted. Action was underway, and it was being done in a calm and concentrated manner. The night's air, gently blowing among them slowly began to fill itself with colour particles accompanied by the faint whisper of dissolving air out their spray cans.

Balwin was the only one of the group who was doing a whole car which meant he had the biggest surface to complete his work on. He drew his line till he couldn't spray any higher, adjusted the barrel beneath the spot where he was forced to halt, climbed knees first onto the barrel and continued his line to the finishing point at the edge of the roof. Although the mounting and dismounting of the barrel was physically tiring, his knees feeling the impact of the barrels rim every time, the atmosphere created by their action was making him merry and content with himself. It seemed the others were showing similar signs, visible to Balwin during their short brakes as they walked to one another to exchange a gay word or two and of course examine the other one's work. After half an hour Balwin was finished with the sketching. The length of the carriage and it's long didn't concern him. Trains in Germany had a similar length back in those days, so he was familiar with the duration of work it required to complete a such in whole. While Balwin was bending over his bag of cans preparing them for his next step, his mind began to shoot up images and pictures of Yankee writers doing their thing on the subway. One figure was assumingly doing a whole car as well by the way he was balancing his stand between two subways on the outer channels, sustaining his hold by clinging one handed to the roofs channel or the ledge of an open window. He could also vision the happy looking young men, like themselves, cuddled in a group and posing for pictures and messing around with one and other. Balwin's lads portrayed themselves genuine in that intimate yard light between the steel colossuses as he looked at them engrossed in painting, cigarettes glowing in and out of intensity with their laid-back attitude rounding the scene up. A style and type of way known to Balwin through his own thriving lust for intense sentiment actions which resulted in sub-awareness and sub-recognition of one's human self, strengthening his personality. Having filled up one end of the carriage, he advanced onwards after his first quarter of excessive filling up the sketched letters with his arm feeling the ache. Left to right, right to left went his arm kept on a horizontal scale at a meter's length with his finger pressing down the cap permanently on the can held in his hand. A couple of breaks from the arm swinging and finger pressing, to ease out the physical tension built up during the half hour and he was finally done with his fill'in. Exhausting he thought but when it runs, oh boy will I be happy. An hour later Balwin stood back, lent both shoulder blades flat against the carriage opposite his and examined his work letter by letter the best he could due to its stretch, wondering if he could satisfyingly nod to himself accomplished. The letters fill'in seemed sufficiently full, the outlines around the letters thick and strong enough to give his piece the effect he wanted it to possess when it travelled down the tracks of the city. That will do he thought, smiling inwardly as he looked at his achieved whole car. It was done at last, his imagination transformed into reality standing impressively big in front of him.

By now so much paint was released that if someone had a guided view across the huge yard to where they were painting, one could see a cloud hanging over them in the air made up from the paint particles.

Looking around himself and thinking where to go next with his remaining cans he made out by examining the other lads, fixed steady to the ground, highly focused and deepened in what they were doing that he could lower his pace. Two hours had passed since they had entered the yard, unimportant actually having to be aware that time existed in the first place relating to the fun he was having. Judging by his inner perception morning would arise in a distance leaving enough night left for more action in the meantime. Balwin separated the empty cans from the full ones making two separate bags.

He decided to procced on to the composition opposite the one bearing his whole car. Two running subways, each with a piece of his on it was certainly better than one running example.

Balwin chose to do the carriage next to the three lads who were doing an end to end made up by their three pieces. Balwin's intention was to do the same but with a singular piece. This meant his letters would form again a piece leading from one end of the carriage to the other end mainly not going higher than the windows.

Walking calmly towards his target further down the roofless passageway, Balwin chilled for a couple of moments aside each of the lads, observing each one's way of working and his outcome and inquired how he was feeling and if all was going well. The response was: "We chill'n big homie, it's under control, taking the time on this background," said Enrique who was perched on the chair creating the background above his piece. Tierra told him once again to take his time, "you in urban heaven homie, you'll be back to earth soon enough," he joked merrily as he smiled full at ease and looking content. In the moment as Balwin agreed giving him a hand clap, he felt while wondering onwards, that everything was fine, and trouble was put at bay. Once again, a lengthy stretch of steel surface was spread out in front of him ready to be transformed. I have to get the proportion of the letters right he thought as he looked at the ever so long appearing space available to him. His limbs felt tired, but that conscious recognition was gone in a blink of an eye as he imagined his proceedings while he withdrew a can for the sketch.

Feeling his energy accelerate, driven by his hungry spirit for continuous action and challenge, he pressed down the cap to let his name free. Moving along the carriage in a relaxed state of being conscious to persist it, Balwin drew his letters mounting onto his toes so he could raise the height of each letter to the arm out stretched window above him. Once again from his left side across his body to the right side of him went his arm as he filled up the letters wide space. Every now and then he stood back for a short brake releasing instantly the resembled air he had blocked in his chest from his strain. Leaning backwards on the composition opposite his piece he regained his breath and a slightly better impression of how his intention was supposed to look like. Looks okay so far. On we go with the outlines and the rest I have in mind he thought while checking out the other movements. The lads had changed places, so he was sure they were on their second piece of work as well which also signalized to him that their night wouldn't be over for a further lengthy space of time. Outlines, background, highlights all was set in place and met his satisfaction he amusingly acknowledged while he admired his second large but not as high achieved piece. Looking over to the others again Balwin became suddenly aware of his present situation as he put his emptied cans back into his plastic bag. He realised that he was now holding two bags of empty paint in his hands. Darkness still remained spread out above them. The only noticeable change surrounding them was that the temperature had fallen to a chill felt by Balwin as he stood in the passage leaning on the subway carriage for ten minutes observing his hosts. What am I going to do now he thought, considering his empty cans? Space for more was all around him and Why-U had told him they would at least be here for another hour or so. The five were now on their third pieces. Come and collect our scraps and see what you can do with them and your left overs said Why-U. "Dam wright homie," replied Balwin and off he went with an empty plastic bag to fill it with more or less empty cans. Now it really felt like being in a Hall of Fame (legal spot) as he withdrew the last drops of colour from the can till nothing more, but air squished out of it. Deepened in painting and concentrated on adjusting the remaining paint to the space he had sketched out, darkness silently began to retreat leaving a grey tone sky that slowly transformed into various light blues with only the morning star and some gliding seagulls left in it. Time had passed with Balwin able to squeeze six, considering the size of the other two, small pieces out of the left overs.

What a night he thought now realising his body's tiredness clearer, as well as the orange coloured sky, there were the sun had entered the out of his view horizon. All six of them seemed worn out but more in a laid-back sense, visible through the expression of satisfaction signs, showing up every now and then on their faces as they came together and exchanged thoughts and their procedures. Why-U suggested he would take the lead after the barrel and chair had been put back in place. One after the other trailed behind the other down the passage carrying bags and the other work support objects. Tierra returned the objects to their place and on they moved out into the open space in stooped positions.

Surely an unfamiliar sight to any onlooker, seeing six crouched humans, belayed with bags scurrying across a huge train depot terrain fixed with hundreds of shiny rail tracks in broad daylight, climbing a wall and then disappearing behind it.

Sitting in the car again with soulful music playing on a reduced level, traveling speed attached to the ease and comfort settling in on the tired passengers, especially among those squashed to one another's corps seated in the back. It felt good to feel the other one's relaxed state of being leaning against you.

Seven hours of train yard atmosphere captured in a gigantic clear over sky space and time disconnected from the world they were now driving through had passed by. Previous empty night streets were now beginning to regain life, filling themselves with early morning movement famil-

iar to nightshift folk, early birds and morning glory prais-
er's. Inside the car silence spread itself among the lads,
each reflecting whatever arose in his mind while gazing out
at the passing world with the soft tone music supporting
each one's self engagement. Possibly intense and profound
or fluttering and enhancing. Balwin's thoughts swayed
through the moments they just spent in that famous yard
with a conclusion arising that fifty cans more would have
done him better. Now I know what is possible he thought
as warming delightfulness swelled in him when thinking of
his transformed wished. His wish went along way he
thought and oh boy what did I see on this excursion all over
town and over these years.

Inhabitants standing on and in the block by their windows
clapping and pointing at our pieces clearly approving our
work as it passed by on the elevated tracks. Transit police
jumping out of the parked subway next to us while we were
painting and enjoying the tunnel atmosphere but were too
lazy to get their act together and come search for us after
we had fled the spot. I was up in a hole in the tunnels ceiling. Half an hour later we were back finishing off our pieces without any further interferences. Or that one time as
we were wading through knee high rubbish in an unused
tunnel when suddenly startled by movements close by
from beneath the garbage. A person arose and fled from
our presence. Continuing our walk more people either
chilling or sleeping became visible. Remember the morning as we were on our way home from some action in a
tunnel, a homeless guy had greatened us and asked if we
had experienced a good night as well. Sure brother. Our
faces and clothes were covered with dark tunnel dust. The
nineties surely weren't clean like New York is today and
therefore not a destination of my interest any more. I can

hola at you like a New York City homie and walk the cypress avenue walk. I've seen one of the cities's intense periods, was accepted in the hood, felt the flow that makes one another feel good, but nah, at the moment eastern Europe is the place that withholds an environment more suitable to me and my interests. It's the vibes similar to the New York City I once knew and surroundings offering a match to my taste I'm looking for. And what pleasures me the most is to have my greatest achievement, my son accompanying me on my voyages into the once used but still existing.

THE STUNT TEAM

Two young men growing up in Graffiti popular times venture out of their European region looking for thrills in capital cities of the continent. Through encounters on their tours they meet up with Paul for the execution of their common goal, the painting of the NYC Subway trains. Their adventure turns somewhat into a sour apple.

Thomas

The last fork full of mashed potatoes, mixed with endive salad was lifted from the plate at the family table and shoved into the mouth of young Tommy. He was eager to get finished with his dinner sooner than later, so he could meet up with his friends afterwards. Once his plate was empty his eyes made contact with his father's, then they switched over to those of his mother. He didn't have to say anything. "On you go son and be back before nightfall". The least Tommy could do before leaving, was to place his dirty plate and cutlery beside the kitchen sink, so his part in the family household was more or less done for the day.

He thanked his parents swiftly before slipping light footed out the front door and into the mild summer evening. It was one of those rare evenings when Tommy got liberated from household duties. Tommy touched by joy, jogged through his neighbourhood towards the small park with the benches he and his friends so often occupied. The boys are on the verge of teenager hood, which naturally blesses them with curiosity.

In the meantime, the four elements of Hip-Hop had settled well in Europe and developed a juvenile culture in most parts of Western Europe. Tommy and his friends, like many other young men in Western Europe are full of interest towards this subculture and are carrying colour markers in their pockets. A scribble here a scribble there. But when the older brothers came along, everyone's attention and pricked ears went directly towards those cool guys. Everything they talked about sounded so exciting. Tommy's a fine built blonde boy. Excitement grew even bigger for him as one of the elder presented him with his own personal name, a proper name meant to be spread anonymously throughout the town he is living in and if eager and cunning enough, even further. No boundaries in particular, except the law, were there to stop him and at that age, if you're having fun, it can be a challenge to break them without getting caught and by the time your once caught, its anyway to late, cause it's your fate to do what you're doing, without getting caught.

The following years Tom dedicated himself to his local town and spread his name with an aggressive attitude on as many walls as possible. Trains weren't an issue to him, because he rarely saw any trains, running painted due to the cause that his town was an end station for cross-country trains, which meant that the painted trains that managed to make the journey to Tom's town, only ended up in the cleaning zone (the Buff). Tom and his friend's teen years were preceding rapidly and the decisions and choices accompanying their age were being made. All his mates chose options that brought them to the big cities of his country, leaving Tommy with his solitary choice of staying behind where he looked after the local business. Time tangled with the wind pushes and pulls the seasons airs across the changing land. Now a strong young man and thanks to his departed friends, Tom began to develop a love for moving steel surfaces with every further visit to their cities huge public transport playgrounds and other graffiti related fields. Also, for Tom after a while his own country grew slowly boring and he ventured into Europe to make his mark on all possible surfaces. Over ground, underground it all got visited and conquered without him ever seeing the inside of a jail cell. Europe's law enforcement troops have other priorities than to go casing after Graff painters, but it does happen. If caught, occasionally you get a slap on your wrist or you have to clean your Tag with whatever kind of cloth you have. Could even be one of your scarce fresh underwear out of your small travelling bag and in the end: would you please leave the country!

Good friends of Tom extended their studies and left the European continent for the famous city of New York. Tom a man fond of his friends and willing to visit them were ever they were, was soon making preparations for a two week visit to the east coast of America with a good native friend.

John
The sun had just past the highest point on its daily routine across the sky of Europe. Every soul and piece of nature felt the suns summer strength, as its rays where free to

shine and warm up the surfaces beneath it. No cloud was capable of maintaining the collective resistance against the gushes of wind being blown in from the sea and from the sea further up north. Below a group of children overlooked by their teacher, where cycling along a neatly tarmacked bicycle lane and they all felt quite relieved to feel the winds strength in their backs, giving them that extra bit of support while cycling. The bike lane was always flat and even, it had no motorised traffic, no hills and no mountains upon its route. Simple fields with grazing cows were flanking the lane as of sporadicly set trees, red bricked farm houses and normal houses. Every now and then, the banks of a canal appeared, and its path of dazzling water lead straight through the whole landscape scenery. The school class was travelling at a reasonable speed, either in pairs or in single file. Johnny, a thin cheeky blonde boy, was observing the long blonde hair, flattering out from beneath the helmet of a female classmate who was cycling in front of him. A pretty one she was, and Johnny thought so as well, but his infancy was the obstruction in letting her know what he thought of her.

For a moment Johnny's attention was torn away from his classmates fine reverse silhouette in front of him. His eyes settled into a cautious stare at a fence set up in the field besides the bike path they were travelling on. He slowed his pace and carefully dropped out of the line, without halting to examine the standing trains and freight-trains located behind the fence. "Aha, this could possibly be a place to paint one of those trains", he thought. Excited by what he saw, Johnny was going to be proud of himself, when he later, after arriving home and having eaten his dinner, would be able to present his discovery to his friends in their park. He doesn't really know what to think about the occurrence, besides painting the objects at the spot, because he's just about to become twelve years of age.

During his absence of awareness towards his fellow classmates a gap had opened up between them, leaving Johnny and his legs to intensify their effort in catching up with the rest of the children.

Previously Johnny as well had received his own name from an elder brother of a friend and like Tommy he was spreading it in an attitude with an aggressive underline. *Fucking shit up* as one can also refer to those certain actions. Later that evening back home in the park, his best friend was quickly convinced by his prescription of what he had seen on the bike tour and a few days later, Johnny and his mate were standing in front of the fence, looking into the train yard.

The two boys standing there on the outside of the fence and discussing what they saw where suddenly distracted by a security worker who came walking along on the inside of the fence. Johnny and his friend after discussing so far, had come to the presuming conclusion, that the dark plastic boxes set on poles inside, nearly touching the fence could well possible be motion sensors. "Hey man, are those boxes sensors" Johnny asked the security worker. "Yes son, that is exactly what they are" answered the security worker. "But won't you set the alarm off, when you're walking around the place"? Johnny questioned further. "No, I turn them off when I'm out walking around and when I'm back in my cabin, I turn them on and everything is active again". "Okay man, that's cool, thanks for the information, you unknowing fool". Now the boys knew how to precede, if they were willing to paint. John and his friend's first steel mission got successfully accomplished.

John, Tommy and the other boys found great pleasure in what they were doing, so one could say: they are the thriving next generation of graffiti writers. The measure for their painting actions was slowly being lifted. Their missions were getting riskier and more intense and on top of it all, the quality of their pieces was becoming significant as well. Literally, the boys were on the verge to hard core.

Beside Johnny's genuine interest towards his free time occupation, his basic education was being more or less unambitiously left behind, which got him expelled from school without him finishing the obligatory school time. It didn't mean John was a total dropout and one couldn't bar him from doing his leaving exams. Like a good teacher should do and it was one who liked him, John was allowed to return for his exams. Maybe a little bit of persuasion was necessary to convince him of the matter's importance. Well, as you may have thought, Johnny boy completed his test to the content of all people involved. The lucky boy even got awarded with a trip to where ever he wished to go. John didn't have to think twice, he knew exactly where his mother was going to take him, and he was the boss of the trip. Everything you wish, were his mother's words, as he named the destination of his desire. New York City was a dream to this sixteen-year-old boy.

Mother and son arrived in Manhattan, both excited and ready to follow their separate interests. Johnny wanted to see subways, street graffiti and most of all the different boroughs with their famous names and different ambiences and flavours. His mother was tickled and electrified by the TV series SEX AND THE CITY, which gave visiting fans the possibility to track down the lounges and bars these women visited in their so envied NYC movie life. Bags got dropped off in the hotel and John demanded to be accompanied to the Bronx. "What the hell do you want up in the Bronx son?" John: "Come on mother, you said, where ever I want to go, we will go!" Under her breath she mumbled to herself, after memorizing: "Samantha sometimes got her inner fire extinguished by a Bronx fire fighter the size of a cupboard, those black pearls." On they went, rumbling along on the subway, past the bowl-shaped Yankee stadium, Johnny glued to the window, towards Norwood on 205 street. For his stay John had set himself one goal and that was his name, tagged up on the outside of a subway train with its picture taken. He was modest with himself because he knew he wouldn't be capable of producing a full colour piece, but a Tag should lay within the realm of his possibility's. The continuous subway ridding eventually got his mother fed up, so she bid him farewell and let him continue on his own. The SEX AND THE CITY bars were awaiting her, and markers were patiently waiting for John to collect them. "Be back at ten o'clock and don't do anything stupid, you hear me Johnno." "Yes mother, no need to worry, I'll be fine."

Into a store he went, where he presumed he would find some markers. John selected a couple, but too his astonishment, he wasn't allowed to buy them. Imagine, he wasn't old enough, but maybe the liquid colour preserves intoxicating ingredients. "Hey man, where can I buy them then?" Salesman: "Two blocks down the street kid, they'll give you a blind eye there." 18 was the required age if you wanted to purchase a marker.

Onto the subway he hopped again, in search of a spot for what he held in mind. Late at night, well after ten o'clock, he had succeeded and arrived happy and inflated with joy back at the hotel, where his worried mother was awaiting her wished punctual return. "Oh, my son, I should have never let you go alone," she sobbed.

Well, he's returned himself safe and sound, plus he's gained himself some new street knowledge to nourish him in the future and he has achieved a goal.

Paul

Our last man to make a contribution to Tommy and John on their mission in New York lives with the name of Paul. His native town lays chained in by one of the cleanest rivers in the world, so pure the water is nearly drinkable, not to mention the pleasure it gives, when swimming in it on a hot summer's day. The water descends from the near Alps clear to see from many places in the town, if you look south eastwards. Graffiti was quite widespread in his town and many crews where occupying the walls of the town. Paul, a young boy just pushing open the door to teenager hood in the year 1999, noticed the activity on his town's walls and he as well felt the urge for adventure. He got started on surfaces well hidden from public, where he experimented with the different materials one can use for Graffiti. The lad was curious, courageous and blessed with a lot of energy, but kept his game to himself, till he really emerged on the radar in the year 2003. His painting style was well developed, and his pieces received attention from other painters in town. That was the way you had do it, where he lived, if you wanted to get anywhere in the Graff scene. Quality, quantity and a good personality, based on high motivation could grant you access to the core of the scene. That was Paul's intention and he made his steps in that direction. Trains were the most attractive objects one could paint and a goal for many painting individuals. The failure quote to reach that goal was quite high and Paul was cunning not to be one of those figures. The available train yards and train depots were split up between a number of painters and the rules that accompanied the activity were well known throughout the town. Thanks to their dreaded retaliation the empowered rules remained respected and were seldom broken.

Paul was able to maintain his patience and obeyed the given rules, which was appreciated by the top shots and in return he eventually got rewarded with a night out to the train yards. That night, Paul embedded between the sleeping trains, trapped in the clouds of aerosol, blinded by the yard's bright golden lights, lost his heart and soul to the joy and sense of graffiti life. His ambitions were set high and nothing was going to stop him. Piece after piece got painted, which made him become a dominate tune on the streets of his hometown and eventually throughout Europe. As for him as well, destinations beyond the continent of Europe tickled his senses. Miami, Chicago lay first on his path, as he made his way to New York, where a friend of his would introduce him to Tom and John, also known as the stunt team.

Paul arrived two weeks earlier in New York than Tom and John. The friends of Tom and John who were living and studying in New York also knew Paul and welcomed him as their first guest. Paul of course got straight to work and did some pieces on the subway by himself and in the company of others. Then New York welcomed the two excited and merry chaps, Johnny and Tom. The two boys, no matter where they are, always try to get the most craic out of a planned trip. So, as they were out strolling the streets of their borough, they bumped into a store with superman bags up for sale. "Aren't they perfect for painting, we'll sore through New York with the power and strength of the well-known super hero." The bags got purchased and were loaded with spray cans. Off they went feeling nearly as confident as our hero, to a recommended spot in Brooklyn.

Paul who in the meantime had met them as well, learnt or heard on beforehand of the stunt team's reputation, as being slightly careless in association with their graffiti activities. So, for himself he decided to miss out on their first common action with the intention of making his own verdict when they came back with the tale of their procedures, just to see how things went for them.

Tom and John arrived at the Brooklyn spot on a mild September evening with over an hour to go till midnight. The declared target lay between two subway stations on elevated tracks. They were told to wait till the subway train in service left the station, then descend from the stations platform and run towards the parked subway train they intended to paint. After that stage they were meant to wait until the subway travelling in the opposite direction passed the parked one. Then the air and tracks would be clear to paint without any further interferences. Both men were highly excited, superman bags boosting their confidence, hearts pounding, and their minds focused on their long-desired task. Down the steps they went, jogging carefully along the tracks, which were placed above the middle of a Brooklyn road. They arrived at the sleeping subway train, poised quickly, pricked their ears and swallowed up the view, overlooking endless Brooklyn rooftops. Well the atmosphere must have been lovely, because they started to paint straight away, forgetting completely they were supposed to wait. Five minutes passed, and the interruption came rumbling up the transit line. Took by surprise, their reaction had to be chosen quickly. The only hiding place available, lay beneath the parked train, where the rays of light from the travelling subway trains head beams, couldn't give the drivers eyes any visibility. Within a second, they were on their belly's beneath the wagon and feeling the gush of air being pulled along by the travelling sub-way. The question now, John and Tom had to ask themselves, do they continue, or shall they leave without finishing their pieces, due to the fact, the driver could have noticed the illegal activity and called the cops. The super-men chose their first option and finished as quickly as they could. At the same time, a slow-paced cop car was passing beneath them, visible to them through the spaces set be-tween the logs of wood holding the rails, but couldn't scare them away. Their decision got rewarded with luck and they arrived home with swelled breasts and appetite for more. Paul viewed their photos and agreed to join them the following night for further action.

A brand-new night began to unfold itself over New York City, calling its creatures to their duties or knocking those exhausted from the daytime into their dreams. John, Tom and Paul had finished a meal and were toasting their beers to a night without any hassle. Caution was the key to a night of success. The stunt team certainly had no intention to become familiar with the ill rumours and harsh conse-quences, New York's law had set up for their felonies.

Their beers got drunken and their choice fell on a Queens based spot, once again located on elevated tracks. This time though, a frequently be-driven highway was flowing right underneath the transit line, giving the elevat-ed tracks, the subway was parked on a height of over forty meters. The plan for the action was to pass the parked subway train they intended to paint twice, encase some-thing peculiar could be seen on the be-forehand. Then climb the bridge to avoid the eyes of onlookers around or in the station, because anyone present was a potential plain clothes cop. Once on top of the steel construction, the subways driver cabin doors were to be opened and the inside of the subway train had to be checked for waiting policemen from the *Vandal Squad.*

On the ground everything looked calm and quiet, so immediately the green light in mind shun up, signalling to them, go. One after another, close behind each other, Paul John and Tom climbed steadily up the steel pillars holding the subway line. The pillars were set together nearly like ladders, making them easy to climb. Anxiety accompanied the three free climbers strain, letting the first pearls of sweat emerge from their foreheads. Beneath them in a constant rhyme, traffic flowed, tickling their nerves additionally. At last the top was reached and through the spaces between the logs of wood holding the rails, lay the entry to the summit of glory. The stunt team slipped through the entrance and crouched down to poise, listen and observe the shimmering silver colossus of a subway train standing in front of them. One set of vacant tracks divided them from the objects surface they were willing to paint. Darkness surrounded most of the subway train, only some pale rays of light shining over from an evenly heighted billboard next to the highway and transit line, produced the main visibility to the otherwise dark surroundings. Still crouching on the tracks, the boys looked at each other and the expressions on their faces told one another, everything till here looked fine and safe. Rising together, they moved slow and quiet towards the head of the subway composition. Now that they were at the door of the driver's cabin, Tom reached out to push down the door handle, but to his and everyone's surprise, the door was unfortunately locked. Whispering to one another, if they should precede despite the locked door, they swiftly agreed never the less to paint. Around the nose of the composition they went and each one chose his place to paint. The space favoured the most lay beneath the despiteful stars and stripes. A photo of your piece, stretched out beneath the American flag can have a symbolic character, meaning, you're (their) rules and restrictions can be challenged and broken. Tom, John and Paul now standing ready, each with his spray can in his hand, looked at each other, nodded and they released their colours.

The sketches were drawn, the letters filled up. In short intervals they paused to listen, if any strange or disturbing noise could be heard, which could signal danger. The boys were painting more or less at the same speed and all three were proceeding on to their background colours, when suddenly, out of a distance a huge spotlight from below, shone exactly on to the carriage they were painting. Startled by the sudden light, the three instantly dropped to the ground. After a few seconds, darkness regained the environment and nothing dreadful was to be seen or heard.

Paul and John who were exposed the most to the light blast, discussed quickly their further actions. Despite the slight tension and insecurity arousing within each one of them, they once again decided to continue.

The three intensified their speed, hoping to gain time for the escape, encase pursuers were already on their heels. Tom, now working on his second outlines, instantly got interrupted by the sudden opening of the door he was painting over. "Freeze motherfucker," while Tom was looking into the muzzle of a handgun, directed at him by a NYPD law enforcer.

John and Paul who were standing a couple of meters apart from Tom, noticed immediately what was happening and didn't waste a single second in reacting. All three turned to the opposite direction of the pursuer and dashed off, running along the side of the subway train. John was first in place, followed by Paul and last in line was Tom with six pigs, grunting and snorting behind him. John really kicked his spurs and began to open up some distance between Paul and Tom. His aim was the next station on the line, which he hoped would be his saviour. Paul who was running in front of Tom made a different decision for escape. He presumed both stations, the one in front and the one behind them were dangerous, because the police surely would be waiting there for them with guns and arms wide open. Paul and Tom were still running, when suddenly out of the pale light a pole appeared in the middle of their path. The path they were running on, was a thin wooden plank, not really meant to run upon, because of the gaps, left and right of the path, which lead forty meters free fall, downwards onto the heavily bedriven highway. An end station for sure. Tom, the last in line of the chase, swung himself, elegantly around the pole with no intention of warning his pursuers. "Smack" the donut crashed into the pole, nearly meeting the steps to heaven for a second. This incident brought his following colleague's to a halt, helping him back to his feet and letting them realise how dangerous their pursuit was. None of them wanted to risk his life for a lousy spray painter, so Paul and Toms escape was made a bit easier. The only chance of getting away, was to descend down the pillars, thought Paul. Through the gap between the wooden logs he went, climbing down onto the kind of steps the pillar produced. Steady, but quick were his movements towards the ground. Arriving at the bottom, he could hear Tom shouting from above for him to wait. Tom isn't quite the climbing type of person, but what other options did he have. Both now on the ground, located in the middle of the highway, they prepared themselves for the next hurdle. Deep breaths were drawn as they peered into the bright lights of the oncoming traffic. Dodge the cars and hopefully make it to the other side. Into the traffics gaps they plunged, bringing cars to a screeching halt, which produced a blockage for the cops picking up the pursuit in their cars on the highway. On and on they ran, despite their poor physical shape they were determined to fulfil their getaway. Running along on the emergency lane, the highway eventually transformed itself into a broad street, stretching itself through a neighbour-hood. Their feet were burning, their lungs were burning, and their heads were close to exploding. Bathed in sweat and lacking further energy, the two lads were glad to have side streets around them, but what the hell was that noise above them? "Tshuck, tshuck,tshuck," went the rotor blades of a helicopter, somewhere over their heads in the dark sky. "Shit" cried Tom in disbelief, "what the fuck, are they serious?" "Quick, quick over here." Paul pointed out a near bridge and into the bridges shelter they shuffled, still breathing heavily. Tom and Paul's faces glowing from exhaustion, rested their bodies under the bridge for over half an hour. In the meantime, the noise from the hovering helicopter faded away and normal night sounds regained their surroundings. One thing the two defiantly knew, was that they were far away from their NYC home and it was still a long way to go.

Sitting there under the bridge, the two wondered what Johnny had done and where the hell had he gone. Did he also get away or were his wrists cuffed behind his back?

John had dashed forward with one thing on his mind "get as far away from those cops as you can." Towards the sta-tion he ran, leaving all his followers behind him. He ar-rived in the brightly lit station, still walking on the tracks and grasping for his breath. Only one person, clothed in baggies and a hoodie was present on the station's platform. "A typical dude out the hood," thought John, so he dared to pull himself up onto the platform. As he was about to do so, the guy moved towards him, pulled out a handgun and calmly said: "Freeze motherfucker or I'll shoot you in the back." John straight away disbelieved him, thinking "he isn't gonna put a bullet in me for the sake of graffiti" and stepped back from the offender. While doing so, he stumbled and fell backwards, but was quickly back on his feet again and began to run towards the opposite track exit in search of rescue. The undercover cop made no intention to follow him. Just outside the station was a pole leading down onto a box from where he could descend to firm ground. Both hands on the pole, legs rapped around it, John slid down onto the box. A bit of climbing and his feet touched solid ground. John saw a fenced in area and in that direction, he once more began to run. Safety maybe lay beyond that fence. Over the fence he went dropping on to his tired feet, his breath pumping in and out as his energy decreased. His eyes roamed over the dark area he just entered in search of a place offering tranquillity. "Hey man, what you doing here", sounded out from a dark object belonging to the sites security ward. Safety was still out of John's reach and he abandoned the site. The only wish John momentarily had was to be far away from where he now was. While walking on the pavement of a residential area in search of a hiding place, a white van appeared further up the street and was driving towards him. Struck by an idea while observing the van, John stood out onto the street to bring the van to a halt. "Hey, please take me along, just get me out of here! I'm being followed by some dubious looking coloured guys." The woman sitting on the passenger seat replied: "You sure, I ain't see any problems around." In the meantime, the driver withdrew a badge withholding the word Immigration Officer. "Show some ID kid", turning on a flashlight and tracing John from head to toe. In the same moment a black van came screeching around the corner from behind and stopped next to John and the white van. The side door opened bringing forth the word *Vandal Squad* and John was quickly surrounded by his pursuers. Again "ID kid," but to John's surprise he had left it at home. A flood of questions got pored over John while his hands got pulled behind his back and cuffed. All John could say was "No" or "I don't know," which clearly didn't please the officers. Now punches were directed at John released by the guy who nearly fell off the elevated tracks earlier. "Come on you fagot, why are you such a coward!" John shouted at his suppresser. "Was it your intention to turn me into a piece of shit," the officer demanded to know. John obviously didn't know what the man was talking about because he was the head of the chase. John's mind spoke out loud telling the cop that he couldn't get much shittier anyway. John got shoved onto the back bench of the van flanked by two officers. Hope was written on the officer's forehead as they drove through the neighbourhood in search of a glimpse of Tom and Paul. After half an hour the search was postponed, and John was taken to the police station. After a quick body check John was seated at a table opposite two *Vandal Squad* officers. Prints of their pieces were put in front of him and he was asked to show them which of the three pieces he had done. John thinking, he was busted pointed out his and didn't provide any further information although one of the interviewers was pressurising him. Typical bad cop good cop show. John was also asked to redraw his sketch and he did it, but knowingly wrong. "Okay mister, you're going into central booking for the night and tomorrow you'll be transferred to another jail." Before being led away, John received a clean print of their pieces from the good cop, which will bring him good fortune later on.

The break Paul and Tom were forced to take did them good. Words were scarcely spoken between the two of them during their regeneration phase. Their further procedure was the main issue that they talked about. On the other hand, both of them didn't really know where they were except that they were seated in Queens for the moment. Energy was regained, and their legs felt rejuvenated and their focus was set on completing their escape from the dutiful *Vandal Squad* officer's and all cops in general. Tom and Paul's plan was to leave the area as inconspicuously as possible and doing so with a night bus. Paul raised himself first then pulling Tom to his feet. Let's try and stick to the shadows said Paul as they began to walk. Behind them lay the highway with the never-ending string of red and white lights. Ahead of them slightly to their right lay a huge construction site with ongoing labour. There were unattended and pretty dark parts upon the construction site meaning they could gain distance unseen. The streets where regarded insecure so they entered the site by climbing over its fence. On they trotted now and then moaning to each other about their tiring situation. A couple of hundred meters ahead of them was a heard of workers all wearing orange signal gear and protection helmets. "How do we pass them", muttered Paul. "I have an idea" said Tom as he walked towards a worker's hut. Picking up a pickaxe Tom drove the pike into the crack between the door and the doorframe. Two strong tugs and the door was forced open. "We'll dress ourselves with worker clothes. That should be the perfect disguise for us two". Thought and said, the clothes were found and upon them a twenty-four pack of Gatorade bottles which also got acquired. Out of the hut they stepped and straight into their new rolls. Two guys entering America's labour force willing to boost the countries construction growth intentions and desire. Well it meant they could maintain their escape route. Pleased with their idea, Tom and Paul merrily continued their walk for liberty. A dull but loud noise most likely from a horn, divided itself across the site signalling to the genuine workers that their shift was over for the night. "Well Paul, we might as well put our shovels aside and join the departing." "I couldn't agree more with ya, me backs done also, enough is enough." Into the stream of lava, they melted passing the main exit unnoticed by the supervisors and straight towards the steps of a waiting public night bus. Smiles were exchanged as they seated themselves in the rear of the bus. Relief and confidence arouse within Paul and Tom as the bus began to move away from their close by crime scene. One thing I forgot to mention was, that before Paul and Tom climbed the fence of the building site they had crossed a patch of green withholding the spotlight machine that had shone upon them during their painting action. A clear sign for a full-scale setup by the *Vandal Squad*. The bus brought Tom and Paul to La Guardia airport where they then changed vehicles. Now they were on their way home at last and seated well on top. The moment they sat down in the back of that taxi, sleep overtook both of them. The taxi sped through the night passing deserted boulevards as they headed for domestic Brooklyn. For forty minutes had the lads been hovering in other realms as the taxi came to its definite halt. The bill got paid and two Gatorades were offered to the driver as well. Barely awake Tom and Paul stepped out onto the pavement still disguised as construction workers. "Who the fuck lets two ugly white motherfuckers work in motherfucking Brooklyn," were the welcoming words from an on looking afro American male. This man's aggressive attitude bewildered Paul instantly and he was in his face immediately. Tom, who was in no mood for a street sprawl just after waking up calmed the situation by pulling Paul homewards. Arriving home at last the long-awaited reunion of the Stunt Team unfortunately had to be postponed.

Instead of lying comfortably tucked away in his bed, John was lying on a wooded bench in a crowded central booking beneath an air shaft that constantly had cold air blowingout of it. John shivering had wrapped himself in toilet paper hoping to receive some kind of warmth. Ten unpleasant hours were spent before John was brought to his lawyer and eventually transferred in a typical American prison bus to a Bronx based jail house.

John was welcomed with the entry ritual every individual inmate had to endure when entering. Clothes off, turn around, bend over, place your hands on your ass cheeks and open up the crack to an officer seated on a chair. "Hey sir, that's a nice job you have there, all day, every day, crack inspection," John cheekily commented. He was allowed to wear his own clothes which withheld the given photos from their previous action. After receiving a blanket John was led to a room where fifth teen other inmates were forced to dwell. The room was quite long and full of bunk beds. In the front part of the room where the entry lay sat an officer behind a wall made out of acrylicglass, observing the ongoing motion. Next to the glass wall lay one vacant bed but Johnny considered not to play the white chicken and headed for further vacant beds in the back of the room. On his way one of the afro American's suggested to him not to go any further back because those Latinos weren't friendly and in spite they might intend to rob him. "I'll be fine, I don't possess anything worthwhile stealing" John replied as he proceeded. Into a bed close to the Latinos in the rear of the chamber he climbed where he then slept for twelve hours straight. Awakening to no particular noise John arose wondering how long his stay possibly could be. Turning to the Latinos in search of conversation he quickly felt his presence disapproved. So, he arose properly deciding to move with his blanket to the front of the room, the light was better there as well. Reaching the front John received a more or less warm welcome from the group of afro American's who told him he had missed his breakfast. But not to worry it was stowed away in his personal locker because he hadn't eaten it. Upon this John was asked for his story. The group of men found it quite unfamiliar to see a blonde white man in such surroundings. The inmates got well amused by his story and signs of respect were directed towards him. John showed them the photos of crime, which then kicked off an exchange market. John drew sketches of anything the inmates wanted. Some were even motives for tattoos and in exchange John received chocolate bars, crisps, cookies and other kinds of candies. They also loved his native country, which withheld many a pleasurable activity, occurring to them. "Hey bro, I got your back, anything you want, hola at me", echoed through John's ears as he sat in front of the telly, stuffing himself with sweets. He was even asked to exchange his phone calls for candy because they were only for domestic use and not authorized for abroad. Latinos in the back, coloureds in the front, bodies were being pushed up and down upon chairs and Johnny boy, the crazy prison hero, was imprisoned amongst this for five days. "Off you go son, your bail has been paid" said the ward on Johns fifth day. Who had paid wondered John as he left the prison holding a brown paper bag with his scarce possessions in it.

Paul and Tom were his financiers, but because a ATM machine has a five hundred dollar a day withdrawal limit it had taken them five days to withdraw the bailout sum of two thousand dollars. At last the lads were reunited over a table belayed with beer to toast to their unwanted experiences. The lads agreed New York had a meaning for them it was an important subway system and if back once again they would do it again.

The New York subways attraction is too strong to with bear passionate subway painters like those from the Stunt Team. But the story isn't over yet.

The guys from the opponent side "The *Vandal Squad*" are passionate lads as well and they use any possible tactic or technique to trace down their suspects. The acquisitions against John had risen to a grand total of eleven meaning the coppers were surely waiting at the airport for him. Despite the fear of that scenario John and Tom still made it onto the aeroplane hoping the threat of a further arrest had been overcome. But no, the *Vandal Squad* officers appeared at the plane's front door. After twenty minutes of discussion delaying the planes departure the pilot appeared wanting to know what was going on in his zone of responsibility. His answer was, "for such a minor shit, everyone on this plane has to wait?"

The cops backed off unsatisfied agreeing to a kind of deportation leaving the judge and his court waiting.

4

THE ACTIONIST

This is a day of action out of our writer's previous life, which transcends into his own history and gradually finds its way onto the streets of New York City in the early nineties.

A noise is piercing through the realms between darkness and the turning World, reaching me in my sleep and bringing me back into the space were everything is physically sizable. It's my alarm clock ringing away at eight o'clock in the morning like I've set it for the last couple of weeks. My time spent behind the lids of the shut eyes with its departed and separated mind, dispatched from the pressures of noticeable time has refreshed and reenergized me for my momentarily daily self-set task. My mind and mood are set and ready and I'm willing to maintain my actions like I've done in recent weeks. But first a French bun and a cup of coffee to steady the engine within me before I join the labour force. On their journey to whatever penny bringing life ring they balance upon. Placed upon my table next to my empty breakfast crockery are markers verifying in colour and seize waiting for me to fulfil their purpose and I place them in my jacket's pockets. Up I get and off I go glancing at myself in the mirror before I step out into the morning seaside air of this harbour city. Looking up at the sky just to acknowledge the metrological situation, which won't have an impact on me anyway, I walk with other commuters to the urban railway station. The city train arrives, and we calmly mount the train's steps, hoping to gain a comfortable place inside. To possibly fix the last preparations in our mental world before our daily required productivity phase begins. I'm looking around myself to see what these male and female images could be nonverbally expressing. I conclude my thoughts with the signs and terms of determination.

Faces expressing certainty, faces withholding firm and stern cheeks beneath even so foreheads. Maybe expressions similar to mine, who as well, as maybe they are, am physically and mentally ready for the essential challenge and in my case self- set duty. In fact, I'm king of my own castle at the moment and not attached to any kind of labour contract.

Our train reaches the next unloading station and nearly everyone moves towards the carriage exit. I do the same and I follow the queue towards the exit but only to halt in the entry and exit section of the carriage where I wait for the doors of the train to close again. Several people are sitting scattered upon the seats of one side of the carriage, so I go back into the empty part of the carriage undoing the lid of one of my markers. Straight to the closest smooth and flat carriage wall I guide the marker and the first of many following Tags gets done. With controlled haste I write my chosen and personalized name in Bordeaux red on one spot of the wall then on to another spot, change over to the next compartment to place it again on the surface above the window. The colour drips savagely if I pressurize the marker strong enough while writing and it trickles unstoppable down the wall.

Then I move onto a space beneath the window, a surface beside the window, crouch down to tag on the floor and eventually arriving at the back and end of the carriage I stop on its wall. All over the wall are these dark red letters with thick drops of its colour descending out of its first given form. The Tag transforms into a new appearance and shape. Looking back at my work before leaving the carriage to change to the next carriage at the following station where I'm going to repeat my actions again. I'm delighted with the fresh but dirty outcome of my interior renovation work. That's what I like and that's how I like it to be done this "Inside shitting".

Day after day during recent weeks, beginning and finishing at the same time I had written or tagged my mornings away on this city's travelling urban trains. Creatively I have destroyed its primary given state. My creations are my personal understanding and taste of graffiti and how things favourable to graffiti could look like. I can clearly see the pictures out of Books from my teenage years displaying the inside walls of the New York City subway. Carriages back then in the eighties were fully covered from top to bottom in tags. Commuters accepted this as their new normality. Those pictures first seen when I was fourteen had thoroughly imposed themselves within me, forming my taste and enjoyment towards Graffiti. Eventually I succeeded with my plan of redecorating the insides of most of this city's urban train compositions. My effort was appreciated distinctively going as far as releasing shock waves of non-understanding. But to tell you the truth that's how it all began and it wasn't Hip-Hop culture that introduced this kind of behaviour to the public and it's plain and single coloured surfaces.

It all descended and began to develop itself out of guitar riff music back in the closing stages of the sixties. Guys in New York and other east coast cities listening to the likes of Led Zeppelin and Pink Floyd had begun to write their names and pseudonyms on walls and other suitable surfaces changing the calligraphy of the letters while doing so. This went on till eventually Hip-Hop arouse in the mid-1970's liberating many a youth from the dull and disillusioning circumstances the city of New York was in at that time. Meanwhile at the end of the sixties over in Europe's major cities, Punk music was gaining a lot of popularity from its young inhabitants and they as well began to write their names or pseudonyms for their cliques where ever they rested.

Amsterdam for example received a fare covering of such behaviour. Amsterdam is geographically located close to my own city and it transferred the same behaviour over to us.

Any sort of name was chosen by the rebellious young folks of that time, which somehow related itself to them or just suited them or simply filled an amusing purpose. Then about ten years later in the mid-1980's Hip-Hop arrived in Europe and its customs replaced the punk tags with Hip-Hop orientated writings. This subculture captured my attention and affection because to me the Punks, Oi Skinheads, Mods including the Teds, which were all separate scenes and they all seemed kind of wrinkled and appeared to me as drained out. They were always around me but when the disc jockeys started to mix in some of those new Hip-Hop songs in the otherwise Punk music discos and we showed our appreciation for its rhythm, the Punks couldn't understand what we were doing and how we could like it.

That's how Graffiti started for me and the accompanying culture goods of Hip-Hop accelerated our visions and youthful experimental actions.

The Punk scenes and before that, the Progressive Rock music wave in Europe and for our Actionist, especially his local Punk scene of his Rhein-Ruhr city had helped loosen the more or less strict and formal social behaviour rules. With their new behaviour and various styles of appearance they had introduced to the following generations new youth forms. New expressions and outlets which allowed individuals looking for lifestyles outside of the given conformities were created. From where afterwards our Actionist had at one stage in his life, deployed himself from the Rhein-Ruhr to conquer the harbour city's suburban train system.

In the Rhein-Ruhr area, Graffiti began to develop itself, throughout its three major cities more-or-less at the same time. Graffiti had made its way out of its cradle and was learning to walk with its strengthened legs. Making and creating one step after another in its infancy shoes, too where Graffiti is today.

We are in Düsseldorf in the year 1984 and the Actionist is breathing and moving since fourteen years. His chosen hobby brought to him through books and movies from the once so dazzling and admirable United States of America. What he and his friends saw and registered out of those informative items, truly inspired and encouraged them to fulfil their following fantasies. The first two years of the Actionists endeavours with colour, from 1984 till 1986, were spent with tagging himself through his town until at the end of those two years he advanced in completing his first lettered outline piece.

Additionally, in those two years his passion for inside train shitting, as one can also call it, unfolded itself and was maintained by him into the new century.

Soon after his first pieces had appeared upon his city's walls, came the longing for more authenticity and so-called *realness*. He had seen Graffiti on trains in the books and movies and that got him and others thinking of doing the same. But where and how was this premier for his region going to get realised, was the question looking for answers. The first painted trains out of the Rhein-Ruhr region although left the city of Dortmund to where they then reached the close by city of Düsseldorf. Showing its capability to the amused Düsseldorfer's and the Actionist.

So, one evening the Actionist and some friends ventured onto the grounds of one of Düsseldorfs train yards not really knowing what to expect, besides a good amount of steel train compositions. Loaded with cans and a portion of positive naivety, the lads on their excursion across the yards ground, bumped into the train's cleaners. Both parties surprised by meeting each other, examined one another and the ones who were clearly meant to be there asked the bunch of young men, obviously false in place to them, what they were intending to do here and why they were here in the first place. "Em, oh, well were just passing through in hope of finding a new short cut home and we weren't expecting to meet you guys," came as a softening answer. The young men hadn't a clue yet how actions involving painting trains were to be handled and brought into a functional concept. So, Düsseldorfs first painted train was delayed. Shortly later the first achieved and functional concept for painting trains got widened and defined in its various procedures. Through their learning and different approaches onto the yard's grounds, the writers of the Rhein-Ruhr quickly gained control of the places where painting trains was possible. Like in many other European cities in Graffiti's early stages, the train authorities did not know how to cope with this new phenomenon. Colourful painted pieces upon trains were running from city to city across the rich coal pastures of the Rhein-Ruhr region for endless weeks, bringing joy and satisfaction to the participating and responsible writers. The writers were lucky that the current situation stayed unchallenged by the relevant authorities which allowed them to continue with their actions on the trains for many a year afterwards.

During the eighties, nearly everything exported from the USA was delightedly embraced by Europe's young and old inhabitants. The range of topics that were sent to the old continent were very wide. We received updates on Sports styles, clothing styles, food styles, music styles, movie styles, life styles and all the information on vehicles. Anything you can imagine was wrapped appealingly for the freshly adapted market and the delivering country was genuinely referred to as Hip and cool by their ancestors on the receiving end. The country was so admired at the time that surely many a European had a visit set upon his wish list for the near future. A book called SUBWAY ART which was published in the eighties took New York's Graffiti activities as its theme. Among European Graffiti writers it became so popular that it created a myth around New York, turning the city into a kind of Mecca for Graffiti writers from abroad.

One of the first to make that visit to the Big Apple out of the Rhein-Ruhr region and Western Europe was our Actionist. He had successfully finished college in 1990 and was rewarded with a trip to New York by his father. This enabled him to fulfil his dream of seeking out the roots of his artistic passion. The journey was granted to him by his supportive father. So, the two of them, father and son, set off to the airport with tickets to New York City. Before leaving, the Actionist had to make some preparations of his own to ensure he was able to achieve his dream while in the Big Apple. He was given a contact address in New York by a fellow German Graffiti artist who named himself PENIS. To his contact address in New York he dispatched a portfolio of his work with a letter of introduction. Unfortunately, no reply was to be found in his German letterbox before him and his father took off to the sky's.

After touching American soil or the surface of those wide concrete avenues, their luggage was dropped off at their hotel and the Actionist pushed on to get cracking as soon as possible. He was anxious, plus curious about his unanswered letter. Had it arrived at the given address and was the content appreciated by the receiver, was the burning question he wanted to have answered. "Come on father lets go to the address I have here, it's up in Queens, Astoria. I would really like to meet this man and see if he has any time for me."

Supportive as he is, he agreed to his sons wish and payed for a taxi taking them to the address in Queens, Astoria. The taxi took them out of Manhattan using the huge steel constructed Queensborough Bridge which lead into Queens across the East river. Reaching the other side, the surrounding environment noticeably began to change. Streets and the housing started to appear slightly worn out and run down. The dark brown bricked houses differing in size and height with dirty pavements were leaving an anxious impression upon his father. They came to a halt in front of a brown bricked housing block with similar coloured people standing around it.

This was the correct address they had been given and both men stepped out of the taxi inhaling Queen's

Borough ghetto air. The Actionist mounted the steps of the block and rang the bell of the required person. Shortly afterwards a big coloured, elderly looking woman appeared at the door and astonished by what she saw in front of her, questioned his ringing. "No, I should be at the wright house if this man I'm looking for lives here. Do you know him?"

It's her son and he got called to the door. Holding an envelope in his hand, the man joined them by the door frame and the Actionist on his arrival introduced himself and his father. "Yes, I am Sasha and I most likely have your envelope right here in my hand. I've just come back home from months at college and have only received it now. Unfortunately, I don't really have the time for you at the moment but I'll hook you up with a friend who will call you later on today in your hotel." Delighted with the developments and feeling slightly proud of himself for making this meeting workout, father and his joyful son left the place again by taxi. Whoa, I'm going to get down with the real deal, it's becoming true, thought our Actionist while gazing out of the taxi's window.

A midst tags and pieces set on all kind of surfaces everywhere around them, were also the area's inhabitants which to our Actionist looked like the real deal. Hip-Hop styles consisting of big sneakers, wide trousers, huge jackets, topped with a fashionable cap upon their distinctive walk. Not a place really to be considered for a holiday outing, except like the father and son were doing from the inside of a cab. It was the life on the block and it wasn't to be underestimated because things weren't looking too rosy in that period in New York City.

The Actionist sat on the end of his bed in his hotel room, hoping and waiting for the phone to ring, while wondering how things would work out for him. He wasn't in possession of any spray cans yet and that phone call was hopefully going to be the door opener to his dreams. A local connection would surely be helpful for all his concerns attached to his stay.

The phone rang and a man introducing himself as *Airone* was on the other end, asking if he was interested in doing some action. "Of course, I am," he replied, and they agreed that Airone would pick him up at the hotel. Meanwhile his father, who was also in the room, was growing hungry but his son didn't want to accompany him to dinner in case of missing his appointment with the dude. Over an hour past and his Father returned from his meal to find his son still there in the hotel room on his own. The Actionist didn't know at the time that Mr. Airone was chronical late and this mostly up to around two hours.

Eventually he arrived, and they got straight into talking and showing one another, pictures of their pieces and the Actionist inquired, whether they would have to steal spray cans to get some action done. "Let's get poppin," he replied and off they went to rack themselves some cans. Happy again with his achievement and "yeah" those cans were stolen out of a hardware store. Shortly after they had acquired them, they literally began to use them straight away. They painted on any available surface that wasn't too exposed in the day times light such as walls beneath bridges. He was flanked by friends of Airone who guided their actions safely. After a good bit of painting and moving around urban spaces came the time to bring up the burning question. He gently inquired if there was any chance of getting a subway painted. "Yes, for sure man, why didn't you ask earlier. But it has to be done by night," answered Airone although he wasn't really into subway painting except for the odd throw up (a quick and simple piece) every now and then. Because his art would be neglected as no painted subway train ran in traffic anymore.

Meaning your piece on the subway went straight to the cleaning depot. So that night the son told his father, while standing there with a plastic bag in his hand which showed dents from the cans inside, that he would be going out tonight to some party. "Yeah right son, that's exactly what it looks like," and off went his son to his appointment.

The plan for the night was to enter the tunnel of the E and F line up in Queens where subway compositions were parked in an endless line, one behind another. Without having to check anything on beforehand the lads stepped down the short stairs descending from the platform and marched off into the poorly lit tunnel. The only thing they had to be cautious about was the operating subway train. Which meant they had to crouch in time beneath the parked subway train they were painting to avoid detection. That was quite a scary act because they had to crawl over a wooden plank that covered the third rail which seemed unstable. The anxiety was heightened because this dreadful powering rail had a couple of thousand volts running through it. Thanks to their caution it allowed the Actionist to fulfil his dreams. A comfortable piece. They photographed their pieces, got everyone ready for leaving and slowly made their way back to the platform. While walking along one could see that the tunnels walls were covered with tags and throw-ups from the previous golden Graffiti years. They were still visible and readable beneath the growing layers of sot and dust whirled up upon the walls by the operating trains. Up the steps they went onto the station's platform and straight into the next homewards bound subway train. Back at the hotel our Actionist invited Airone to come upstairs for a soda but the night warden wouldn't have any of it. Couldn't blame him really because the two of them were covered in dust and dirt and didn't really look like they belonged to this hotel and that's what the warden told them. The Actionist pulled out his doors key card and they were let in. "What the hell happened to you," asked his father seeing the state of them. "We were at a camp fire down by the river," answered his son. "Cut it out, you can tell that story to the fairy's. What happened?" he repeated more concerned. "I've painted a subway train in its tunnel." "Have you gone totally bonkers now my son?" was his slightly angered response. "No father, but it was the greatest experience I have ever felt in my whole life."

Despite his honesty towards his father, there was much more going on around him which would have concerned his father to a greater extent. The spirit hanging over New York at the time wasn't comparable with Düsseldorf life or even with today's ways of being in New York. And the Actionist was getting a fare insight of how things occurred around Airone and his friends Disney, Chester and three-5. Firstly, the young men were always armed and poised for combat. Hassle and stress could be lurking at any given time and on any given corner block. The lads weren't gangsters or ruthless criminals, but still, a baton or a knife, some pepper spray or a knuckle duster would help solve a problem likely to happen on their paths through their city.

Criminality was at a high level in 1990 in New York and they couldn't feel safe where ever they went. Aware of the vulnerable state some places were in, the group of friends ventured into those spaces, taking advantage of the given situation. They were able to paint subway station walls and no one standing on the platform took a blind bit of notice. Painting during the day didn't seem to bother anyone, depending of course on where you did it.

One day Airone took the Actionist to the famous Harlem Hall of Fame which was a place where you legally could do your Graffiti pieces. The walls were covered with pieces of high quality or simply said: there where good styles. While they were looking around and admired the pieces a man appeared advancing towards the two of them and he introduced himself as *Gato*. "Who are you?" he inquired directly and in a harsh tone. "I'm Airone and this is a visiting friend," he replied giving the Actionist a side wards glance. "You're that bitch outta Queens," and while Gato said that he lifted his shirt and reached for his gleaming silver pistol. Instantly Airone pulled out his can of pepper spray and sprayed the burning liquid into his face. Over noises of pain he told Gato what he thought of his act and the two scurried off more or less running for their lives. Once in safety they had to catch their breaths and Airone told the Actionist that this was daily business. From behind them arouse the noise of people shouting and they turned to look what was going on. It was Gato again heading towards them accompanied by five determined looking men. Shit, the heat was on again and the two were forced to regain their pace if they wanted to avoid the confrontation. Down the pavement they ran changing street sides by sliding across car bonnets that were brought to a halt through their rapid intervention in traffic with their pursuers close on their heels. Seeing a nearby taxi, the two headed for it as an answer to their salvation. Tearing open the cars doors they literally fell into the passenger's space and while tumbling in, commanded the driver to hit the gas as fast as he could. Slightly puzzled and not quite understanding the reason for their petrified command till he, the driver himself, saw that shiny silver pistol emerging towards his cars window, instantly understood the urgency and they sped off in search of sanctuary.

Sitting in the back of the taxi, sweat was pouring out of his body while observing, New York's life moving on the pavements below those dark brown bricked blocks. The Actionist could hardly believe how exciting and intense his holidays were developing. New York seemed to be a vivid and wild place with a lot of hidden intensity within, that wasn't finding the right channels to relieve it's energy.

Back home in Germany were everything was moderate and Hip-Hop with its four elements was in its experimental phase, the Actionist on his return was mocked by his friends. Them saying, that his achievements during his stay in New York were surely close to zero. "Listen up boys, who did the New York City subway? Yeah, not you or you but the successor of the Rhein-Ruhr, me," was his gleeful answer.

In the following year the Actionist returned back to New York accompanied by his friend Mason. Thanks to his first visit everything was set for ten days of straight painting. Hardly anything was seen of the city except for tunnels, yards, walls and the inside of a jail cell for stealing spray cans. The Actionist, who was the one who had been caught was standing in front of the judge in the court room. He was supported by a state appointed lawyer who had to deal with all the days cases. The Actionist was asked by the judge what his plea was, guilty or not guilty. "What's going to happen to me in both cases," he required. The judge to him: "Well how much money is in your wallet right now?" The Actionist: "Em, I need ten for the subway ride home which leaves me with eighty dollars, sir." – "Bam" the judge's hammer landed on its mat and that was the punishment. Eighty dollars in cash. Off he went, a young man in the early stages of life not feeling concerned in the slightest. New York was still a crazy place which allowed spaces for people to express themselves.

The next year, once more back in New York, love had woven it's enhancing string of feelings within the Actionist and he was towed towards its source. Back again in the city of dreams, this time for three months, his time was taken up by the woman he met. No painting just the satisfying bond of her presence. The challenges love withheld for a couple over took his body and mind. After his love affair New York didn't see him for eleven years.

In the year of 2004 he returned to the city where he had experienced so many wild and stunning moments. He was flabbergasted to see the immense change the city had undergone. All were forced to cooperate and convert too it. Many houses, buildings and places he had once known had been demolished and replaced, inhabiting global operating companies. On every corner were the boys in blue, preforming in an macho manner. Another kind of Disneyland based upon capitalist consummation was won through freshly orchestrated advertisement. Willingly, people unknowingly were carried away by the newly formed rhythms of consumption. He had arrived at the centre of globalisation and could as well have stayed at home.

Two years later he returned once again and accomplished a new piece on the New York subway despite his awareness of the authority's oppressive attitude towards Graffiti and his own advanced age. Over all the years of him prowling through New York's subway system maintaining his youth's inspiration he had achieved a respectable amount of work upon those silver colossuses vital to New York's citizens. Sadly, though he never succeeded in observing his own panel running on those funky tracks and only gained a glimpse of what the Graffiti scene had once been back in those erased golden days. After all his visits to New York he found the Graffiti scene he had been seeking, in Chicago. A trip to Chicago in the late nineties had satisfied his need. Here he met the core of a vivid underground hard-core subway painting scene. They were defying the oppressive tactics of the local authorities to achieve their goal of self-defined spirit which lead to satisfaction through acquiring and accumulating freedom.

To close this story the greatest acknowledgement the God's from the Olympus of Graffiti could grant a participant like our Actionist, was to guide his painted panel upon the Roman subway network, safely through traffic for a whole decade.

LUCA ALONE IN NEW YORK

Passion and commitment, caution of his capability to self-fulfil his aspirations. True to himself the best he can.

As a day in the year 1991 began to unfold itself, my younger brother was up and about the house following me to my various stations of body hygiene, enjoying his freedom of movement. It's lovely and comforting to attract his attention, but I'll gladly have the crap house to myself, small fellow. The youngest member of my family, my sister had woken my parents as they told me later at the table with sweet self-communicating gurgling but because neither of them attended her it turned into cries and eventually flowed into tears. That's when I woke up, lying a floor higher, hearing my parents comforting her gently and responding to my brother's inquiries. He was insisting to my father that he wanted to go to the forest again which grew behind our house which literally also forms the cities western boundary as well as my neighbourhoods. The fir trees begin to grow in the distance of a stone hurled by my father's strong arms. I had finished my breakfast; my school-bag was packed and ready to accompany me to school. "Time to step out on to the streets of my neighbourhood." Depending on the weather I would walk or cycle to school. On my path through the houses and streets of my area, something new to me, had caught my eye. Upon the walls of our unit of housing, built earlier in this century for the labourers of nearby industrial expansion as well as outside our estate on walls running along the tramway. Letters scribbled next to each other in a stylish way, which then formed words. These words repeated themselves on all possible surfaces. Most of the words had meanings, but why were they there? Sitting at my desk, lost in thoughts and unaware of what the teacher was teaching, I noticed that my schoolbooks had lots of vacant spaces and pages, which I then began to fill with words of interest to me. I also tried to form the letters differently; to the way they were written on the blackboard in front of me. More of a curl, stretched them in length and played with their sizes, till I was either disgusted or delighted with what I had created. This scribbling and drawing was raising a desire within me and my courage eventually persuaded my desire to put my chosen name or word up, up on a available space in public, anonymously. Classrooms and years were attended and put behind me, while my interest for these scribbling's and colourful lettered pictures maintained itself and grew all along with me, in the recent years.

We are in the year 1997 now and I had learnt from an elder brother of a friend who confidently was doing what I will shortly do more often, that the colourful lettered pictures were called *pieces* and the scribbling's were called *tags*. The (side) walls flanking train track's, unattended schoolyard walls, walls that weren't to exposed to the eye of man and woman, had let me achieve my first colourful pieces.

The afor-mentioned brother of my friend introduced us to the local urban culture store in my native town Berne. I discovered besides the cool clothes, the various genres of vinyl and in front of the racks of spray cans, laying on the counter, magazines with black and white pictures of pieces on trains. I was amazed and astonished to see that the range of paintable surfaces had just been extended in front of me. "Painted trains, wow, are also getting used for the purpose of Graffiti." Never had I seen a painted one running around town or on my local train line. As these pictures, withholding train pieces got touched by colour, my eyes left my mind even more impressed and fascinated by what I had seen in those magazines.

All of a sudden, walls were retrieving out of my thoughts as I searched the urbanized train mobility zones I knew of, while I shifted my metal work file back and forth, not to precise due to my wandering thoughts. I was giving the joint parts of a metal hand railing it's wished clean up ordered by my apprentice master of metal works. New fantasies of me painting trains were erupting within me and soon my will, eagerness and determination led me and some friends to the places these huge colossuses of steel with wheels where resting, when not in service.

Loads of knowledge and information were gained through dozens and with time, hundreds of successful attempts in putting my name on whatever wheeled steel I came across. Graffiti, one of the five elements of the subculture Hip-Hop, was taking me all over Europe. Graffiti had sealed a tight grip on me and I was devoting most of my time and energy towards its customs. I was part of something significant, significant enough that it rewarded me with acknowledgement, respect and secured confidence within me. The fact that Graffiti can accelerate a reached goal was pushing me further into the depths of Europe's major cities. Winding tunnels with dimmed golden lights, dirty from top to bottom, abandoned, old and belayed with train tracks and electricity rails were laying ready for me. But how does one join the people who are familiar with painting these *Metro* trains? (Subways as they are also called?)

The first time I was granted access to tunnels was in the summer of 2003 and believe me, the experience blew my mind away. It was a totally different surrounding for my pieces and the action was new and exciting. The atmosphere in the tunnel, filled with electrifying air engorged itself in my body. Anxiety and joy were brought together, setting free adrenalin rushes that I had never experienced (on previous spraying missions) before. Graffiti's grip was sealing itself firmer and developing a kind of addiction in me. Metro's were rated the most valuable surfaces to paint on, within the graffiti culture scene and I was eager to join the hunting and collecting of Metro systems throughout Europe.

2009 had dawned and it was time to go back in history and give the birth place of Hip-Hop culture a visit. New York's Metro, called *Subway* in the Big apple, was the prototype of Metro painting. It can be viewed today as a prestigious subway train model, trapped with nostalgic memories of Hip Hop and graffiti stylism.

"This is it," said the graffiti artist repeatedly in the world-famous Hip Hop movie STYLE WARS as his painted train pulled slowly into the subway station for him and everyone else waiting there, to see. A moment of magic to every train painter, spurred by the painter's curiosity for satisfaction of his or hers previously done work. Now it's my turn and chance to get my name up and running on these, to me, must do subway trains.

At last my holiday's would start, one day of work left to do and few minor preparations had to be made, before I could board the plane to New York. I'd given myself ten days for the visit including the painting business. First of all, I followed the path of a normal tourist. Walks through Manhattans overloaded canyons among the flow of pedestrians, down the grand, yellow dotted avenues and out onto the so familiar Brooklyn bridge. There I went to view the most famous skyline in the world.

The impressions that I collected in the first few days were somehow, slightly unreal. Nothing was really new to me. To many times have I seen movies based in New York and the screen it was shown on, was like a window with New York moving behind it. I could be sure now, that if I was to get arrested during my main reason for being in New York, that at least I had seen the official highlights, for the case of being expelled from further visits to the USA. Rumours of a hard and unforgiving judicial system had spread over Europe and for this reason I gave my stay a good planning. The adventure could unfold itself on my command and I was ready to blow the horn for my solitary hunt of these silver sparkling uptown, downtown subway trains.

I commuted like a local across the city, in search of a work place for my actions. A vulnerable spot had to be found, providing an accessible entry to a subway depot, also called *Yard* or *layup,* located either over ground or tucked away beneath the ground. My first target, that I had declared possible, was a boat ride off New York; reverse the entering passage for immigrants a couple of hundred years ago, to the Island of Staten, Staten Island. Upon the Island lay a small outdoor Yard, tightly fenced in with barbed wire, so fierce, it would drain the blood out of your body, if a blade pierced your flesh.

In a quiet hour of night, I slipped through the fences weak spot to place myself between the sleeping trains. No soul was about, and the high posted lights gave enough visibility for me to work and I was intending to start straight away. Out came my bag with the spray cans. One was set in my hand, so I was ready to get going after a short pause with pricked ears, to ensure myself that there was no trouble coming my direction. Go. The pressure from my fingers released the colour and I sketched my letters neatly beneath the subway's windows. Again, a quick pause, so my ears could scan my surroundings for any sound of danger. Nothing could be heard, accept the faint screeches of seagulls flying above me. The pace of my heart reduced its speed, leading me into a steady rhythm, in which I comfortably filled up the sketched letters with the colours I had chosen for the fill' in. But what I saw in front of me didn't please me at all. The colours I had placed in the letters were running, running, dribbling down the side of the train. "Well there's not that much I can do," shot through my mind. "Just keep on going and try to work as clean as you can."

The spray cans I am using are called KRYLON and nothing to compare with European cans. For fear of meeting the New York graffiti cops *Vandal Squad* in a Manhattan based graffiti store, I had decided to buy them in a Hardware distribution centre. No jar headed, wanna be Nicolas Cage should get in my face and ask questions about my stay and intentions in New York. The rumours in Europe describing the *Vandal Squad* where present in my head, so I took all the necessary precautions I could.

On I went, picking up the next spray can I needed to

draw the Outlines around the filled-up letters. The drips from the layers of paint I had sprayed upon each other, weren't bothering me anymore. Right in that moment I was just happy and content being able to stand where I was, and tip toe left and right of my piece, creating that long dreamt dream. Confidence was warming my body, letting me know that the city of dreams should withhold enough options for improvement.

Time was running, as well as my piece. My painting debut in New York had an elastic time limit of maximum twenty minutes and I felt that the deadline had slowly been reached. Swiftly under the guidance of my calm hand, the last of my lines were drawn. Pure white, gleaming as highlights should, upon a Graffiti piece. Well not that bad in the end, was my inner comment as I poised to suck up the noises from my surroundings. I let loose the flash of my camera and made my way back through the yard where I had come from.

Our worlds light and comfort planet was proceeding with its daily routine, spilling weak, infantish light, that gained strength by the second, casting more and more light across the darkness of the Atlantic ocean and reflecting back from the giant mirrors of Manhattan.

The ferry pushed gently forwards, past the seemingly blindfolded statue of liberty. While passing, as I was dazzled by the rays of sun, she had given me a hint that I was right in taking my own liberty.

Everything was prepared for my next goal and this mission was going to get framed and hung up somewhere in my home, my personal mark on a historical piece of New York.

My chosen target was in lower Manhattan and it provided a double track layup yard right underneath the famous

Broadway. The spot I had chosen was slightly peculiar to me. Above the yard on the ground levels surface laid this destruction site of the twin towers that was the cause and promoter of more restrictions, regulations and intensified surveillance for the world's population. Which hit public transportation, our playgrounds, the hardest. The subway station I was heading too, had a station ward and the female wards attention was directed in ease at the monitors in front of her. She is sitting in a wooden box near the main entrance to the platform, with windows so broad, she was on display. I assumed she was watching something entertaining, which would have left me scratching the back of my head in disbelief. Upon the platforms, not one soul was to be seen and that meant our station ward had nothing to see on her cctv screens. On the other hand, I was startled by the total lack of surveillance cameras all together. Aren't we in a city protected by the constant, permanent level orange on the terror scale? Well, I suppose the threat ain't that serious, if basically anyone can go for a walk in the tunnel. If they are aware enough of the details in the surroundings.

Above me, Broadway lay in its night time mode, scarce scattered Hot-dog stalls with their vendors standing by, dreaming of that door with prosperity behind it. There were also hardly any cabs about and luckily, not a copper insight or neither anything threatening to my project. This usually busy part of New York, for once or every night, except the weekends, was deserted. What I had seen made me feel quite confident and if everything went well, I knew my mission would turn out to be perfect. Once again, I had prepared and planned every detail in advance. I knew exactly which part of the subway I was going to paint. The reason being, that when my piece pulled into the station the next morning, it would stop in the best possible spot for me to take photos. Fifteen minutes was the maximum time I had to get my business done and this period of time was between the operating subways. On I moved past the unaware surveillance officer onto the platform just out of the reach of the scarce station cameras. I went along the wall of the platform towards the tunnels entrance. One calm glance back over my shoulder to secure my ongoing feeling of confidence and swoosh around the small tunnel gate, down the five steps and here I am at last. New York's old tunnels leaning on ancient steel pillars and dimly lit up, free to walk slow and smooth towards those silver colossuses. No irritating noise touched my ears as I moved, nearly tip toeing towards the spot I picked for painting. Time is important in this moment and my clock said: the operating subways are soon due to arrive in the station behind me. From where I am, I can see back into the station. Only one person is waiting on the platform in this lonely hour of night for the subway to take him to his chosen destination. A faint rumble is emerging from the depth beyond the station, letting me know the subway is approaching. I'm kneeling between two subway carriages, so when she passes for the next station I'll be out of the driver's sight. Here she comes, lighting up the tunnel with light from the passing windows. Out I crawl from my hiding place and I'm standing beneath the stars and stripes attached to the side of the carriage. I look left then right, everything is fine and out of my backpack come my spray cans, this time purchased in a proper can store way uptown.

Quick but steady the letters L,U,C,A find the surface of the subway. On comes the colour for the letters fill-in, straight afterwards the pieces background, followed elegantly drawn by the letters outlines. Now the second outlines are required as well as the gleaming last but not least, white highlights. What a nice rhythm and flow I'm in and thankfully without any disturbances. "Whow, it's looking very nice and clean, just a bit strange it's my own name I'm looking at." You're a good lad is what I'm feeling. All the cans are back in my bag and I have roughly two minutes left to get out of the tunnel and back onto the platform, without anyone noticing I'm entering the station from a restricted area. A last glance back at my self-homage and what I saw made me poise for a second. To me, its urban scenery, both beautiful and mystical and a mind and soul challenging experience as well. A final draught of subway tunnel air and off I went, homewards for a few hours of sleep.

During my walk home through a quiet New York the whole action passed my mind and left me thinking; have I really done everything I wanted to do on that piece or had I forgotten something? A slight twinge of anxiety arose within me, causing me to doubt my work. No, it can't be or have I for once forgot my highlights? They've disappeared out of my memory, I'm really not sure at all now. In that moment I could have sworn out loud, but no, what's the point, I'll go back and do them again if there not there. Shit all this risk again. Round I turn, very aware of the time I had left. If I get there soon there will be a good chance that no one will have noticed yet, that someone had trespassed.

Around four in the morning I'm back at the station, but before I enter again, my attention is directed towards the on-going procedures in the street and on the pavement. My eyes and mind are wondering across the spaces for any sus pious behaviour from possible counter observers, plain clothes cops or god knows what else. Luckily enough Broadway in this section is still more or less deserted and calm. Into the station I go, just with my white for the highlights and my camera for the photos afterwards when my subway goes into traffic. There is also the possibility that it will take off from its resting place and only stop when it reaches the cleaning depot. I'm moving the same way as I did before, the warden is still focused on one of her screens and the platforms are empty. Looks like luck is on my side and I enter once again the veins of New York. The next subway due to arrive is about in five minutes, but not to worry, I'll be finished and out again by then. My curiosity is at boiling point as I, approach my piece. LUCA is still there and upon him, yes, the highlights as well. Why didn't I remember this time out of all times. It's the first time in my whole graffiti career that something like this has happened to me and on top of it all why in New York, have mercy with me. I heard a faint rumble, so I ran back to the steps leading to the platform. Before mounting the steps, I noticed that two people were standing on the platform, "fuck," but if I emerge calm and peacefully, they'll hopefully mind their own business.

I board the arriving subway, so it can take me to the next station where I hope to get my traffic pictures. The time has come for my subway to appear for its day's work, but no, what's going on? Maybe the driver or some workers from the MTA transport have discovered the intruders colourful work and they're now discussing what's to happen with it. All I can do now is wait. The subway has to leave its resting place if they're going to clean my name and the subway has to pass the station I am waiting in and with luck it will stop shortly before it takes its final journey. I've planned my mission so carefully, but I'm not totally in control of the situation. Subway Graffiti only helps you presume what could happen, but you don't know exactly how things will precede. Patience, flexibility and improvisation are valuable virtues in this arm of Graffiti. After thirty minutes of inconspicuous waiting the two high beam lights of my subway, eventually press slowly forward, towards me into the station. Here I am, straight in front of me, what a lovely feeling it is, to look at my name Luca written nice, clean and clear on the shiny silver surface of a New York City subway train. Discreetly I join in with the onlookers and take pictures just like the others. It seems they liked what they saw and so did I.

Is that what one could see on the side of the subway train, reminding onlookers of the New York back in the days when every single subway carriage was painted from top to bottom with colourful pieces and scribbling's? To me those days are gone and how things are developing at the moment, they surely won't be back. But at least it's still possible to paint under reasonable conditions and it's twenty years on. I'm happy and proud that my contribution to the past went so smoothly and successfully for me, leaving me wiser and richer in experience for my future.

CROSS CITY TROPHY HUNTERS

*A story hoisted out of memories pond, spun together
many years after it happened. Their will, hope, patience
and courage maintained their search for joy through
completing.*

Good evening chaps, it's a great pleasure to have you all
here and I must say, how wonderful it is that our worlds
have brought our lives together again after many an autumn, winter, spring and summer has passed through us.
Summer has come to its end, the weathered green is
changing to sunburnt brown in the leaf's preparations on
the branches of its tree for their annual departure retreat,
slowly but determined to complete the trees naked arrival
on the year's shortest day.

We are here in my living room on this autumn
evening, seated upon couches that are unfortunately worn
down to the wires because I didn't want to believe the state
the second-hand furniture was in when I bought it. The
style of the couch had won me over quite instantly. Coun-

try house design with thick dark blue cotton linen adjusted decently upon it. "Excuse me, I'll be chucking them out as soon as I can." "Not to worry," says Rafid, "but it worries my back." The room's high built windows are kept open thanks to summers well persisted hang on. The noise of thin traffic can be heard from below swaying up into the room accompanied by bird's chatter. We are all comfortable to see one another and only these three men as soon as they correspond to their common adventures, which I admired out of a magazine as a teenager, know and feel the intensity of life embraced in memories that arise while they tell their tale.

"Big Pun has died," mentions Tarek somewhat puzzled after picking up and understanding the phrases shouted out across the pavement and street by an evening newspaper distributer standing at the top of the staircase of a Brooklyn subway station. It's a cold February evening in the year of the Millennium. "Oh, he was a gifted rap text writer who wrote for Fat Joe the other NYC big poppa," says Malik to Rafid and Tarek. "Yeah, he sure felt the hood and the circumstances life circulated upon. A true channel of speech," continued Malik. "Wait, I think I remember a phrase off him: 'Ever since I was young, I wasn't always Big Pun, it wasn't always this fun. Ayo, I rose from the slums.'" I wonder how big the burger set was he took at White Castle. "He probably had a double thirty or so," added Tarek. White Castle is a Hamburger chain that sells tiny Hamburgers slightly bigger than a jewellery ring box. The unique thing about them is that their not offered singular. There multiple stuck next to each other. The smallest order starts with a pack of six and always doubles up. Rafid points at a Police vehicle that is parked further up the street. "Look at that it's a fucking police lorry.

Everything out of proportion over here," continues Rafid, as they walk next to each other on the pavement with the Oceans incoming breeze biting their cheek bones. It's just gone eight o'clock. "At last some peace and quietness, nice to have some space around one's body," says Tarek as he sniffs in the salt touched air. The hectic back there in town isn't really my thing and boy those people are seldom strange, everyone seems stressed. Tarek chatters on. "Nutters, all nutters and those writers what the hell are they up to? It seems like no one is painting anymore. I'm on nightshift, can't do anything. My girlfriend will kill me if she knows I'm painting. It's too hot here in New York you'll get your arse busted, fuck that. The yards too far away from where I live. Oh, yeah we still paint. Yeah in the shops backyard." All these excuses.

"One thing you do see is *Cope 2,* he's everywhere," says Rafid. "Yeah that's true, he sure is present." Tarek goes on in a dry tone. "The *Vandal Squad* is probably out and about pestering any area showing new Graffiti activities with their scare tactics. So, lads soon we'll be there."

Malik looks round himself and peers into parked cars saying "I hope the bloody Squad ain't out around here and keep an eye out for people chilling in cars." "I don't think any of them would be hanging around outside. It's too cold," replies Tarek. Malik is a tall slim guy and a cheerful communicator. Rafid is also of slim stature but has grown shorter than Malik. He persuaded Malik to come along to New York City. The three of them are heading for the Coney Island Subway Yard. It's not really an Island but it's Brooklyn's farthest out to sea part with the Belt Parkway making Coney Island with its long-stretched sand beach and amusement Park easily accessible from Uptown Brooklyn and Manhattan. Tarek is broad built and roughly the size of Rafid and is the groups guide. He's already been here in New York a couple of times and knows various painting spots all over town. The three are staying in New York City for three days and tonight is their last evening. Nothing so far, has been painted but especially Tarek is convinced that luck will be on their side tonight. Everyone is eager and determined to achieve something paintable. The will, pumping through their bodies and moving their legs is bundled to one energy ball of striving motivation. Outer circumstances and interferences from Officials will be the only counter powers to stop them from painting.

As they walk along Tarek explains the procedures necessary for them to make before they can enter the huge yard. "We're going to mount the subway tracks that lead pass the yard. They are set behind a Hospital complex on a ridge with bushes on its side but there's a path for the unofficial workers leading through the thicket. The tracks are set wright next to the fence of the yard and in one spot of the fence there should be a hole. Let's all hope it's not fixed and don't forget lads, the subway trains are still running. That'll be our entrance to the sleeping room of the B, N, F, Q and D lines. I think all lines can actually go for repair service in there. Once in, we will first have to walk along the tracks then scurry across some open space till we reach the trains set in file and in between we go. We'll wait a short while for a reaction to our entry and if nothing occurs *da nan an nan na nan na nan* smack that shit up." Rafid mentions that a cutter would have probably been handy, just in case for the hole, but never mind we'll do it without. "Where can we get our cans ready," asks Malik. "Up on the tracks. We'll be out of sight up there," answers Tarek. The three go quiet as they walk along each dwelling in his thoughts. One thought is most likely shared among them, "I want to paint." Aside the back street their walking on, Tarek points at a strip of bushes at the end of a small parking lot set next to a smaller building from the hospital complex and announces their arrival. Nothing suspicious has been seen until now and Malik the last who pops into the bush searches their surroundings a last time. The path is muddy slippery and warningly steep and the three are wearing runners. So, cautious boys or one will be sliding into the other behind him. No one wants to get wet and mucky. Moving cautiously forward Rafid's foot slides out of grip; his heart makes a jump, but he can adjust himself by widening his stand on the ground with his other foot. Malik behind him chuckles seeing the movements in front of him and holds his own stand for a moment. The path is poorly lit and so are the tracks they arrive upon. Visibility is provided by the yard's lights high up on the poles, but they light more or less only the inside of the yard. The three prepare the contents of their backpacks. Caps are put on the cans and instead of shaking them up and down to move the paint inside preventing it from having an Overkill, they get circled to keep the noise down. An Overkill can happen when it's cold which makes the colour inside the can block the output when activated because it's too thick. Malik is ready first. "Do you also hear the noise from the shifting around subway trains?" he asks. Dull sounds of steel clashing together get carried through the air accompanied by screeches from the subway trains wheels as they sway left to right during their motion. "Come on boys my toes and fingers are feeling the cold," he says.

A couple of moments later Rafid and Tarek are ready, and Tarek takes the lead again. Step by step is placed on the wooden logs which stabilize the iron tracks hold on the ground. Their walking along a double line of fence with Nato-barbed wire attached on the top. Looking through the fence an amazing amount of Subway train

105

compositions can be seen in the distance gleaming under the orangish yard light. "Wow," says Malik overwhelmed by the sight. "It's gigantic let me count the noses to see how many compositions are parked there." "Go on," says Tarek. "Me and you Rafid, will keep an overview of what's going on inside. And after you've counted we'll go for the hole." Rafid mentions, that over there to the closer to them side of the yard just behind the parked trains, is movement. "Looks like subway trains are getting uncoupled and moved away," says Tarek. "I've counted 45 compositions," says Malik bewildered. "Imagine a hundred more writers here and the outcome in the morning. Beautiful I would think and afterwards everything running. Boy the commuters would be happy." "Passed is passed," says Rafid, "but one never knows maybe one day again." They move on with Tarek taking up the lead again. "The hole should be here somewhere," says Tarek. I'm sure it was close to one of these poles. Ah here it is, smiling as he points it out to the others. He also looks up and down the tracks they are standing on to make sure no subway train is advancing. "Hold the bags in your hands," he says and bends down to his knees to crouch his way through the hole. The other two intimidate and are standing next to him between the two fences. "Bhmmm, bhummm" goes a horn from somewhere nearby and they duck instantly to their knees again. "Fuck, shit," are their responses. Malik stretches himself up slowly to gain a glance from where the noise could have come from. In that moment the headlights from a subway train composition parked close to them goes on and the visible driver shouts something in their direction. A few moments later the subway train moves into motion and descends out of file. Three tracks away the train passes, and the driver signals the horn again. "Bhmmm, bhummh," goes the uninvited sound off up into the heavens and across the yard to the operating tower and beyond, but out there beyond cares no one.

Instantly struck by the interference the lads look at each other while crouched on the ground and Tarek nods with his head in the direction of their coming and says quietly, "we have to go. The tower has also heard it and we don't know if the driver has reported us over radio." "Sure, let's stay on the safe side," agree Malik and Rafid. They retreat hastily taking sometimes two logs a step moving as quick as they can back to the parking lot. Just to be sure they have a self-comforting feeling of having a lead on the possibly alerted *Vandal Squad*. After a while of walking with the temperature freezing in the minus zone, Rafid proposes to get a bite before they mount the subway again. "Where are we going anyway now," he asks Tarek? "I'd say Flushing Meadows, it's up in Queens next to the American Open tennis centre. The place is smaller and has an entrance like the one before. We will be able to warm ourselves up and regain some energy on the ride." Up ahead a couple of burger chains, clearly visible through their energy consuming name signs, are neighbouring each other but Rafid spots a grocery store instead and chooses a ham, egg, cheese on a roll please, served hot. There's always something going on in those stores and the people speak with the sweetest of the city's accents.

Just before they enter the subway station they decide to board the subway each alone and then meet up again in one of the carriages. Three young males in a group, the way they were looking, all carrying backpacks could just appeal to a *Vandal Squad* officer who would be posted around or in the station on the lookout for the possible suspects after being alerted. Swinging in one hand the paper bag with the food in it, each walks the best he can, in a residential way through the station ignoring the other nearby himself.

The station ward sitting comfortable in his heated booth is nibbling on a chicken leg with a jug of fizz drink next to his meal bag. He's absorbed and gazes at the pass byers as if seeing a fleet of Viking boats approaching beyond them. Rafid, Malik and Tarek meet up in the carriage and seat themselves in a row of orange seats. "Quite a nice model," remarks Malik. "I like the channelled side work. To me it makes the subway train look older than it is." The three eat their roles in silence in a more or less empty carriage. It's ten o'clock and the subway has come from the end station. Rafid looking at the subway map unfolded in front of him tells the other two that it's going to be a long journey. "We're going through the whole of Brooklyn with one change and onwards up north into Queensborogh with a further change." "How long do you think it's going to take us, Tarek," asks Rafid. "You can go to sleep if you want. I'd say two hours." "Count how many stations we'll be passing, Malik," he continues. "No, I'll do it," says Rafid. Some people enter the carriage, all are tucked in thick jackets and wearing head gear and beneath those baggy trousers surely, they'll be wearing a second layer of something. A man wearing a cowboy hat presents himself in the standing section of the carriage and begins to pull on his accordion. "Soy un rangerooh en el ciiiudad e buscar un amorrrr, tu eres para mi mi mujerrr." The man's probably from the old California judging by his looks. He even has a colourful pair of cowboy boots on his feet. Maybe their passing underneath a Mexican neighbourhood in Brooklyn. Many different communities live in Brooklyn and the other boroughs of New York, sometimes even with their heritage language written bilingual on the area's signings. The man sings and sings, sways slightly sideways while pulling on his instrument, summoning from the depths of his belly strength in his voice during the deep tone parts of his tune and slowly lets the emotion burst out in the long-stretched words on higher tones. A lovely scene for our three lads who aren't really familiar with this kind of entertainment but observe it with admiration. The subway stops, doors open and half a minute later the door closing signal alerts briskly and they continue after the doors shut with a thud. From behind them, further back in the carriage a high-pitched yawl mixes in with the music on display and on turning they see two other men in a similar appearance carrying guitars. "Wow, hopefully their going to play together," says Malik seeing that they know each other. Rafid interrupts mentioning cool the number of stations that are still left to pass. "40 lads, lucky we have a show on in here," he smiles. "And when do we have to change," asks Tarek. "12 more to go, Tarek. Do you like the music?" questions Rafid. "I'm not familiar with it but I must say he sure is expressing a longing out of his depths," answers Tarek. The guitars meddle in with the accordion. "It's lovely to have some live music and their playing well," he continues before leaning back with closed eyes head tilting against the window. The triplet are playing songs called *La cucuracha, no se a manana, por un mujer como tu* with one of the guitar players doing the vocal parts in a calm and soft manner. Less powerful and enthusiastic than the accordion player. After passing four stations the triplet splits up and approaches the other passengers using their cowboy hats as baskets. Some give some don't. Each of our three lads donates a couple of dimes and quarters. Malik even thanks them and wishes them a good night. Engine noise surrounded by the rattling of the traveling subway regains the carriages inside and makes up a dull acoustic. Irregularly the light in the carriage flickers and distinguishes but once the wagons back in contact with the third rail it's on again. On they go. Rafid announces the station of their exit. Time to change lines after forty minutes.

Sitting aboard their next subway Rafid asks Tarek for a story from his previous visits. "Well two are popping up in my mind. Ones to do with painting, the other was a funny coincidence with other painters. I'll give you the co-incidence story and you'll agree with me that it's always special when things like coincidence happen. It makes you wonder about the world and yourself attached to the word why. I was out in Manhattan in a shoe store with some guys from a town near yours when all of a sudden, my two mates, while we were discussing the style grade of a pair of shoes that were waiting to get bought, won the attention of two lads in our age by yelling at them across the store. The whole store looks startled our way. We don't care and the two lads grinning come over and it's a happy greeting. My friends introduce to me BUSY and LEVEL from the GHS crew straight out of Berlin. I'm like 'pull the building down,' wow how cool is this, of course I know you two and your crew what a pleasure and honour to meet you guys and on top here in New York. We didn't have to ask them what they were doing in town and a short while later we were up in the Bronx hitting a subway train on elevated tracks at three in the afternoon. What a jam and then they were gone. That was so special to me. How magical it was and how lucky I was mate and them from that crew and by daylight." "Sure would have loved it as well," says Rafid.

Malik asks Tarek some questions about the place where they're going to. The subway rattles along some-times jolting side to side when changing tracks in full speed with the carriage semi occupied. Is this a normal evening ride? The light flickers and goes off for a couple of seconds. People going home after work, after a Broadway show, a Knicks game, a rendez-vous dinner? Or anyone just woken up? Off to work, off to some entertainment, transporting drugs, following the heart to another heart? "Well we're going to paint your city's subway," thinks Rafid as he overlooks the inside of the carriage checking the people. "How long," Rafid asks Malik who is slowly becoming impatient. "Imagine you live in the subway Malik, dinner time now. At least uuhmm, it's nice and warm." "No no, mister Royce daa 59, two more stations to go," answers Rafid now standing and swinging himself lightly back and forth on a crossbar.

"Come on Tarek, time to wake up. You'll have to put that dream aside for a while. We want to make a dream come true now," says Rafid in a motivated tone. "I was dreaming that the subways were parked in my back garden and I was first swimming in the nearby river, then painting, back and forth full sports till now." The subway comes to a halt and the three exit the carriage each on his own and by a different door. The first thing they see on disembarking are parked subway train compositions with their roofs reflecting under the yard's overhead lights on the other side of the platform behind a big sad looking fence with a second one behind. In between the two fences roles of Nato-barbed wire are laid out. The yard is right next to the single platform station. Tarek indicates with his hand hanging down beside him for them to follow him. Slandering behind one another two meters apart they head for the end of the platform. The subway train passes them into the darkness with only the lighted windows left to be seen in the distance as it moves on a curve out of sight. Not many people disembarked with them and no one suspicious had awaited them. Reaching the end, knowing that the platforms deserted by now, they jump down off the platform onto the bed of tracks. Tarek tells them to follow close and to carry their bags in their hands again. Off they dazzle towards the fence, bodies bent in hope of being less visible to anyone present nearby. Along the fence they run in the direction of two compositions parked right behind it, 100 meters in distance.

"The hole should be at the end of the compositions,"remarks Tarek hastily as they jog along. Everything looks calm on the other side and the building standing parallel to the subway trains is in a state of darkness. Tarek aims straight for a spot in the fence but on looking turns around uttering swear words. "It's sealed," he says kicking into the fence loosening another string of words interesting to a teenager. All three disappointed, examine the fence and the quietness the subway train is resting in. Malik reads a sign attached to the fence close to where their standing: *Dogs on guard. No trespassing.* But none are to be seen or heard. They all agree on the spot that they'll have to go and look for a 24-Hour store that has fence-cutters on sale. They're convinced that some business should be nearby with the item available. "We're in twenty-four-seven country," says Tarek maintaining a determined voice. They return to the platform before a subway train arrives and exit the station through a passage leading to a plank way cutting straight through the yard but above it. It's a pedestrian bridge leading to the neighbourhood surrounding the park and tennis court complex on the other side of the station. Off they go in search of a hardware store in the middle of the night. Just after leaving the bridge behind them Rafid for brings the wish to hide their bags. "We shouldn't be walking around the streets with our bags on, what if we get checked," he says. "They'll have us sleeping on a wooden bench, plus we'll be buying new flight tickets." They find a hiding place.

For one and half hours they wonder through streets with scarce traffic about and even less foot movement on the pavements. Looking down the streets in search of the stores sign of desire somewhere up high between the housing blocks, one can otherwise see steam rising into night air out of the sewage holes placed in the street or one's own breath erupting and disappearing in front of oneself as one searches the walls of the surrounding buildings for signs of interest and direction. Every now and then a hardware store does appear but it's closed due to its size. The only stores open are laundry hubs, 24/7 grocery stores and take away diners. Sometimes an open retail chain appears but on searching its contents the wire cutter is missing. Luck doesn't seem to be lurking in this area of town so they decide to give up and move on in hope of finding a place obeying their wishes. Once again, they mount the city's accelerator and through the borough's they travel fully aware of the plentyness of stations lying between here and there. Going to bed definitely isn't an option although their tired and moving upon weakened legs. Too strong is the will and inner energy inside the three, retightening its bundle while they sit next to each other awaiting their next arrival. After checking the possibilities available to them far uptown beyond the island of Manhattan, with luck lacking a warm welcome on their curious inspections there as well, Tarek proposes his last accessible location for their trip. Hours have past midnight, hundreds of miles of tracks have been travelled upon and their riding down the Manhattan Island certainly the last time tonight or obviously now, this morning. "I think the place where we're going now is under construction so I can't say it's going to work out right but if we're lucky we'll be in a warm place with great circumstances," says Tarek. "Ah Tarek, you sure know your spots and we've had a great experience so far. I mean all those yards we've visited tonight and we were always so close. A last try won't do us any harm and it's on our way home isn't it," asks Malik in a weary tone, his face expressing sincere determination.

"Of course, Tarek we've travelled so far and we're all still motivated, lucky for us we were able to sit half the way," adds Rafid who is sitting slumped in his seat like the other two next to him. Tarek focuses on his friends. "Okay then lads, 15 stations to go and let's not forget to be very cautious about the travelling subway trains when we're walking around in the tunnel. We'll be underground and the morning traffic is just beginning to pick up. We ain't got much space along the side walls of the tunnels. Every couple of meters there are little shafts we can press into when a subway train approaches us. Stay behind me and the rest you'll see."

After travelling half the night with the subway stations and carriages mainly to themselves, tags were placed on the inside walls of course, commuter space now slowly begins to get reoccupied. Afro Americans and our three Europeans weary and stained by the night's excursion were now being accompanied by whites and latino's which meant they had entered upper east side Manhattan. Nearly everyone at this stage of the morning has the, got out of bed face confirmed with quietness. Our three lads looking around themselves interested in the mimics of the days phase tried not to be obviously starey and acting too foreignish. "Lexington Avenue: change to express for downtown," mumbles the driver into his microphone as the subway train reduces its speed before entering an orange tiled station with a narrow platform.

"This is it lads, time for work," says Tarek in English rising first to his feet before the train comes to a halt. They get out accompanied by a couple of early morning labourers and follow the signs leading to another platform from another transport line a flight of stairs deeper down in the earth. Walking out onto the platform a strong draft swishes through the station signalling the arrival of a subway train. "Oh, am I happy," says Malik briskly that the air is warm down here. "Imagine the temperature the wind was like outside. It would take the hairs of your spine and you'd have an ear ache bothering you to sleep later on. It's nice and cosy here in the warmth and the situation looks just fine now that we're so early," continues Malik. "The best is to come," says Tarek who marches off towards the end of the platform and the tunnels entry on the far side of the station. A subway train arrives twirling up air as it comes to a halt in the station and same as above a few people descend heading for the stairs leading upwards. The subway train regains motion and disappears into the darkness of the tunnel. The station that by now appears to them as if it had been under construction because the walls don't seem very permanent and the platform as well as above is very narrow. Tarek addresses the two. "Okay fellows, when the last person is gone up the stairs, you follow me and the last of us checks the platform once more before we go into the tunnel. Let's stay close to one another and if a subway train comes, we press ourselves into the shafts in the wall. Off we go!" he commands, and they head for the tunnels dark opening in steady step. Rafid who is last looks behind himself as Tarek pushes the *Entry forbidden* sign aside and walks down the four steps leading off the platform and into the tunnel.

All three are down on the tunnels surface. They pause quickly, look at each other and Rafid nods to Tarek to move on. They scurry off into the tunnels stretch staying close to the wall. "It's not far," says Tarek loud enough so both behind can hear him. A breeze begins to pick up and in a couple seconds it turns into a draft becoming stronger and stronger. "Subways coming!" shouts Tarek and jumps over the single line track heading for a shaft on the other side of it. Malik pulls Rafid by the coat into the nearest one on their side. They turn face wise to the wall, Rafid pressing Malik into the shafts corner, the side the approaching subway train can't see them from. The composition roars past them creating a light vacuum in which they can feel the subways weight dragging at them as it hushes by. After it's past they look across the line to see Tarek moving onwards again. They cross the tracks to catch up behind him. They are jogging now. After a couple of yards Tarek comes to a halt and points at something in the concrete wall. On looking they see a square hole on knee height there. "On you go, Malik," he says, and he moves on his hands and knees through the hole. Malik can feel as he moves forward that the wall isn't thick. He moves into the pitch black. "I've got a light," says Tarek from behind. "Just stand up and wait till we're with you."

A minute later sparks fly into a flame and Tarek holding a firelighter is standing next to Malik with Rafid by his side. Their standing in a square concrete room the size of a small bedroom. Tags fill the walls. "We have to prepare our cans here," says Tarek and they begin to unload their backpacks and shake the cans. Important, no one wants an overkill. In the corner opposite the entry hole stands a small oil barrel. "And now," asks Rafid after their all set and done, "you got dynamite with you or what Tarek?" "Ah no, my friends we just have to put the barrel aside and on doing so a further hole appears. Come on lads on to your knees again." The room turns dark again. Crawling hands first through the hole their hands come in contact with the cold iron of the track, so each knows he can resurrect himself. "Now we walk back again," says Tarek and always remember, we have to be very quiet so we're sure no one in the layup hears our approach and if lucky we can hear them first. They're walking back in the direction of the station they just came from but on the other side of the tunnels wall. Tip toeing along in the dark nothing is to be heard except their movements. In a close distance ahead of them two red lights come into view and judging by Tarek's arm waving figure in front made visible by that faint light, it must at last be their long hunted source of motivation.

On seeing the angular frame beholding the two red lights each of our lad's excitement begins to grow bigger and the blood circulation within their bodies accelerate. Tarek who was uncertain at first about his final idea, insecure that the subway train wouldn't be available to them is now primarily happy to see its massiveness awaiting them there in front of them tucked in industritonicly between iron rails and concrete walls. His nerves thump slightly as they reach the nose of the composition parked aside a deserted and seemingly abandon platform. Standing beneath the impressive front of the silver metal New York City subway train with its service line letter and driver window set above them. It's the model with the channels on the front and the side. He signals to the others to chill. The platform is sufficiently illuminated by bulbs dangling on short cables and as Tarek puts his head around the corner of the nose to have a look what's on it, they clearly hear the arrival of a subway train on the other side of the wall of the platform. One can even hear people disembarking and the clattering of their shoes as they walk along, so yes, the wall is as thick as a wooden plank and this place must have been used differently at one time or it never fulfilled its constructed purpose at all. It could well be that the platform is divided in two and where they are standing, is the unfrequented part of the station. "All looks fine," he says as he turns and faces Rafid and Malik. "We're ready aren't we?" he asks and tells the two to get going on the first two carriages.

Each places his bag on the platform and pulls himself up onto it. "If anyone comes, he'll be coming through the door over there in the wall or from the other side of the train. We run back the way we came and although it's looking easy, let's stay alert," says Tarek calmly while withdrawing a can from his bag.

"I'll paint here," says Rafid pointing to the surface beneath the transportation emblems and destination plackets embedded on the carriage. Malik favouring the same background for his piece, goes to the other end of the carriage which also withholds the plackets. Tarek settles himself on the following carriage next to Malik. Above his piece the location of execution will be clearly visible as well. All three embrace the feeling and possibility accompanying their action of having Graffiti's origin titling their pieces. "Standing on a platform in a warm tunnel with its unique smell in the sticky air, good light conditions, a grand model beholding the famous signing and people one likes to share the adventure with, it couldn't be better, what a trophy," remarks Tarek sitting on the sofa thousands of miles distanced from New York and many years away from the occasion but by looking at him, he's seemingly back their right now himself. The lads paint for half an hour, each taking his time to get his best done. Nothing dangerous signals its advance, no hurry is required. In this moment all three are content. Each fellow's focus is drawn to what he is doing, arms executing the flow leaving *Syer, Alive* and *Scor* behind on the subway trains side. Home sweet home is where they are standing in these forever lasting moments. Once finished, out through the door in the wall they go onto the platform, up the two stories of stairs and out into the icey morning air with sun rays tickling their eyes as they emerge out of the ground. Straight away they disappear into the flow of business men and women dressed posh and speckles clean striding to their pulpits of profit maximization. Buildings soring high, the days braking buzz everywhere and feeling like the centre of it all, our happy and hungry lads, by now physically exhausted enter a diner for the new day's meal.

This story made its way from a bench in a train station set beneath Europe's eternal Kings, the Alps, rising high behind their backs as they sat and admired the daily passing Intercity train from Milano to Brussels. The reason that won the attention of these two young teenagers Rafid and Malik as the train passed, where the endless colourful pieces, top two bottoms, tags and whole cars on the trains side. They were barely 15 and already aware of Graffiti's existence and doing a bit themselves in close by towns. Pieces on walls where okay but not too fancy and accurately tangled please. Graffiti simplified referred to as bombing and this on rolling steel seem to them more so the real deal which they eagerly learnt to pursue and succeed upon. Meeting Tarek a couple of years later at a Hip-Hop Jam in another part of their country, him who also had the finest experiences with painting steel and a similar attitude as our two, bonded in common interest sharing afterwards the pleasure of spreading Graffiti nationwide. Tarek belonging to the country's steel lovers avantgarde tells us, that New York Graffiti lifestyle had once lived in our yards. Mainly on weekends back in the early 90's, here in this small central western European country. On weekends bunches of people, even bringing grills for barbecues with them beside ladders, stools and bag loads of cans would paint day and night, train row for train row till they looked just like New York's subway trains back in the 70's and the Intercity from Milano passing through the mountains on its way to the sea.

THE RASCAL

Five young men travelled with their Interrail tickets towards the east of Europe in search of Graffiti adventure. The Rascal, who had met some of them previously was their host in Bratislava. He had helped establish the Interrail painting culture among Graffiti writer's. The youths journey leads to the Rascals realm of action crossing over into stretches of his tale. For an intense start to the culture the five finish off their tour in Budapest.

The chilly cold of the night which settled us with shivers more or less from the moment we stretched ourselves out on the mattress placed on the grass. The first rays of July's morning sun swiftly chased away the cold. The shivers had been so intense I wasn't able to make friends with sleep that night. Although we had come across a decent looking mattress in a dustbin container located in an accessible ground floor room of a hotel building the softness it provided couldn't make up for the biting cold that night. We lay next to one another under the torn off sheets of advertisement papers seeking sleep and comfort.

Rising one and a half hours after day break, gaining warmth from the sun the two of us set out for Vienna's West train station in order to be reunited with three of our friends who we had been separated from the previous night. Undercover police had noticed us enter a Metro yard and come to check us out. They discovered us in our hiding places, probably because we weren't the first to have hidden there and they began to follow us who had just noticed their intention and made off walking casually down the street after dropping from a five-meter-high wall aiming to gain distance and anonymity. They caught up with us and one after another was summoned into the police car and taken to the station for inspection and investigation.

Three of us were released together and made it onto the last Metro of the night into Vienna's city centre. Of the remaining two, one had jumped into a bush to hide himself while the other had got arrested. They bumped into each other as the one fellow sitting in the bush spied him coming down the street past midnight after he had been released. The two wondered through empty streets for ages in search of a peaceful park.

Arriving at Vienna's West station, with its wide-open space covered with tram tracks set into a nicely mowed lawn. We past under the stations building corner tower to meet our friends at the baggage compartment. Happy to see each other we embraced retold our stories cracked some jokes about the coppers, one of whom had been an extremely attractive woman. We checked the timetable switchboard for our departure train leaving to Bratislava.

I think we were all glad to leave Vienna that late morning due to our misfortune and inability of getting a Metro painted. The prospect of meeting up with a cunning young man calling himself *Rascal* who had held out an invitation to us some months earlier reshaped a fresh hope and sense of a successful adventure ahead of us. Walking up the stairs leading to the train platforms the grey and white Slovakian intercity stood awaiting its passengers with a good spirited conductor suited up and inquiring friendly in which carriage we had our seats. We didn't have any reservations and there were certainly more than enough vacant compartments to be occupied. Having taken up a compartment for ourselves we quickly settled into the soft covered and well silky cushioned seats. The train slowly began to gain pace as we past Vienna's buildings leaving the station behind us getting quick glimpses of moving life in the streets in between. The heat out and inside the train was quite extraordinary for us youngsters who had never experienced anything like it before. Pushing down the compartments window we weren't familiar with 35 degrees plus. We collectively relished the constant draft of cool wind gushing in creating a libertine air for all of us to relax in.

Passing the city's last buildings whilst looking out of the window one could see outstretched in front of us the vast agricultural plains as flat as the surface of a calm ocean. The sky above is blue with seldom bunches of cotton looking clouds drawn together here and there. Somewhere beyond this sea of nature should appear further towards the east the capital city of Slovakia.

After an hour on the tracks some of us grew restless and began to walk up and down the gangway in search of something of interest. One of us had brought along for the journey a square end key which fitted the locks of most train doors. It was meant to yield an entrance into train carriages in case one needed a dry sleeping place for the night. Having produced the key to his friend who said, he would use it to look into some cupboards on board. We told him not to act stupidly and to take care. We didn't want anyone falling off the train. Some minute's past and he returned nearly jumping into the compartment with a big smile on his face. "You won't guess what I just found in a cupboard by a door." We tried to guess, was it: A gun. A dead rat or a briefcase? "No something that me and him nodding at one out of the four like but haven't brought with us. It's an amazing bud of skunk lying there in a tiny pocket bag awaiting its long-delayed consumption." There was quite a bit of dust on it. The two of them got together and rolled the green herb into a Spliff lighting it up in the compartment and puffing the smoke directly into the constant drag of outgoing air. As the Spliff declined the two sitting next to one another turned silent leaning their heads against the head cushions and gazed out the window. Commenting on the inhalement the two declared it light and easy going. Outside a big river came into sight flowing parallel to the train tracks. Looking out of the other train window a rusty factory plant appeared down trodden and abandon. One of us who was in mobile phone contact with the Rascal informed us that our host unfortunately won't be awaiting us on the platform due to labour commitments. He advised us to spend an hour or two in the train station or its surroundings till he arrived.

An hour and a half have passed since the train has departed from Vienna. One of us called for the rest to look in his direction. We saw on the horizon grey outlines of seemingly never-ending buildings stretching into the distance. That must be Bratislava the five of us agreed after one of us had consulted his train ticket for the arrival time confirming our assumption.

Drawing closer to the grey outlines the concrete

squares grew faster and faster rising into big flat and high faces with thousands of small square eyes set neatly in file from left to right and bottom to top. Passing by the housing units with their similar shapes beside the tracks they found no end. It looked like a lot of people lived there. Our train reduced its speed pulled into a train cargo site passing numerous wagons in various forms awaiting their voyage to manufacturing centres. A couple minutes later, station platforms came into view with signposts bearing BRATISLAVA PETRZALKA on them. We collected our rucksacks and made our way to the trains exit. Disembarking from the train the heat lay sweltering in the air sporadically eased by a gush from a cool breeze blowing amidst the empty station platforms. The station didn't appear to be one of the busiest ones. Entering the main station hall, we got greeted by gleaming black and white marmot floors and walls with hardly a soul about. What were we to do now was the decision we had to make? There were a couple of hours to ourselves before we were going to get picked up.

We decided to lock up our baggage and only take some plastic bags containing spray cans for a walk along down the train tracks.

Occasionally we saw people crossing the train tracks where it suited them, so we were convinced no harm would be done walking aside them till we found a spot for some easy pieces. And so, was it. We came across a bridge and took our time painting its pillars while feeling at ease beneath it. Otherwise we enjoyed each other's company making jokes and sharing our thoughts. The hours passed by with our curiosity growing as of to what lay beyond those walls of housing.

A text message arrived, and we were told to meet our host at the spray can store in the city. Having collected our baggage from the station lockers, after a quick group photo in front of huge alien looking locomotive nose we headed towards the bus station located on the other side of the cargo yard. Lacking portable internet, it hadn't really come into existence yet, we asked people waiting for the bus if they had heard of a Graffiti shop in town. Luckily a young chap knew what we're looking for and explained how to get there. "Thanks mate," and an hour later we found the shop and shortly after our arrival the Rascal entered the shop and we rejoiced warmly. He told us he couldn't quit work any earlier but we contently waved off his apologies describing our time spent in the meantime. The Rascal laughed heartfully to the tale of our pleasant occupation. He was dressed in a short-sleeved shirt, buttons opened down to his belly button added by swimming togs and to cover his feet he wore trekking sandals. We spoke in broken English together which proved to be sufficient for our collective understanding. He was in a fine spirit and spoke calmly and was always good in attaching a joke to what was being spoken. We were told to buy cans for the night but before that he'll take us to the gravel pit lake where part of the town would be enjoying a sunbath and a dip in the refreshing water. First though we went off to his house to drop off our luggage.

Walking in the direction of a tram station we passed through the old town of Bratislava which consisted mostly Austria-Hungarian buildings just not as posh as in Vienna. Towering above six story buildings viewable from most places in town lay the well-preserved castle set on top of a hill. We reached our tram station which was situated on a wide pavement with an easy-going flow of towns men and women. He informed us that unfortunately, his city didn't have a Metro system. The city travelled by tram and bus and of course by car. And if you wanted to go beyond our town the train can take you to nearly every big city and town in the region.

Being born in Bratislava and adopting to his surrounding and community the Rascal during his time in elementary school around 1997, became aware of the ever-growing number of tags in his surroundings. Quick to discover that the suspects were familiar to him he put himself forward saying that he would like to add his tag and presence and to be involved. Markers and spray cans got organized no matter the cost or no cost. Funding was hard to gain for the Rascal like for many other young people but sometimes a job would come his way. The basics of Graffiti got dealt with and throw-ups, colour pieces, bombings and tags emerged.

We left the city's centre and the tram began to accelerate and sped along a broad boulevard sharing it with other vehicles. Big patches of grass supplemented with trees of different sizes came into sight interrupted in regular intervals by lengthy grey and light-coloured blocks of flats. Nearly every building withheld a silver or colour piece on its side and a good number of them were familiar to us.

Graffiti belonged to Hip-Hop when it arrived here but he the Rascal didn't enjoy the accompanying music. Back in the days of growing up he would spend so much time outside. Football, Basketball, Eishockey and girls were his primary activities and Graffiti just added on wonderfully. Like most kids they interacted a lot with one another and their neighbourhood created a good environment to support their will for encounters and engagement. The Rascal with age began frequently to create spells of longer absences from his classes. Too exciting and tempting were the options away from school. Him and his friends were now painting trains. This activity could be done by day and time was made available for actions and socializing with other likeminded people who like himself scarcely had any money in their pockets which limited their opportunities. Of course, they discovered ways to fulfil their desires. Bratislava as a medium sized city has a handful of train yards which were already being used for Graffiti activities. It was new terrain that the Rascal was expanding onto and not all were happy with his ambitious approach and appearance in the files of train compositions. It was the year 1999 and in fact one chap was quite pissed off with his interference. His attitude couldn't refrain the Rascal and his friend's eagerness to share the train yards and their running pieces. A couple of months to a year passed by and friend after friend began to drop out of the painting scene till in the end only he the Rascal was left. He was willing to continue on his own. Living in Bratislava with his mother he occasionally wondered to what his friends had turned their interests too, and why he himself remained content and fulfilled with what he enjoyed doing.

Having begun the 21 century our athletic conscious living Rascal gained support from a fellow painter from the city of Praha. This comrade invited him to visit Praha with the prospect of trouble-free tunnel expeditions and Metro painting due to the severe flooding the Donau had caused the city's Metro system. Tunnels were flooded, electronic security systems were inoperable, which literally meant the Metro carriages were vulnerable for painting. They set off to Praha with both of their minds full of goals and determination. The two gripped each other's palms and struck a bond of alliance. This act completed a common ground for friendship resolving in a pair of Rascals. Moving about in Praha they discovered painting options above and below the surface of the city which withheld promising new domains, challenges and thrills as yet unknown to the bratislavian Rascal. The pair acted to their fullest abilities and painted numerous whole-cars, top to bottoms, panels plus they even manged to do a whole train piece. This new field of action impressed both of them. The summer floods of 2002 in Praha set the course for the Rascals boat to voyage off the current of the Donau in pursuit of places and city's appealing to a travel hungry mind.

Our tram rattled to a full stop and the Rascal told us group of lads that we had to get off. We were loud and laughing a lot due to the jokes and jabs we aimed at each other. Every time an attractive lady stood near us or passed by the Rascal engaged himself in a talk or he tempted us shy boys to ask what we wanted to know from her. We weren't too secure about ourselves and were glad to learn and observe how the Rascal did it. Crossing a wide patch of grass which lead to his unit of flats we arrived at the ten-floor building from the back. The surroundings on the backside of the block were spotted with trees and the grass was up to our ankles. The high rise casted a shadow across the orchard like space which created a cool summer air after the straining daytime heat. Two of us met his friendly mother while dropping off our bags at his place. The other three continued their walk to a friend of the Rascal who lived close by. Meeting up shortly afterwards we had our swimming togs and towels under our arms and were off to the gravel pit. Now our curiosity sharpened as we wondered what kind of bathing experience was awaiting us. Seemingly at the pit the girls were at their best: they'll charge us down just to enjoy an ice cream with us joked the Rascal. They absolutely love tourist people said the Rascal now topping himself with a red cap with a white cross embroidered above the fore head. "Certainly, they'll be all over you," he continued, "just approach anyone you like."

He didn't know that we're not to experienced in womanizing let alone being able to get the words right. We arrived around dinner time and people dressed for the beach were walking towards us. Walking along a path which lead up a stone ridge we came to the top overlooking a bowl of water something sized between a pond and a small lake. Men and women were swimming. Kids were playing on its shore and shored a short distance off land was a barrel platform with youths jumping head first off it. The waters grey colour sparkled in the evening sun and appeared inviting like most waters do. Looking across the bathing pit, over in the far end one saw electricity cables hanging concerningly low over the water. Losing a worrying thought, our home country had strict standards, it was more so the dangerous looking picture it produced which concerned us but none the less our clothes came off and we tumbled into the refreshing water wading about playfully. Every now and then the Rascal and a local friend tried to persuade women to spend some time with us. The lad's approaches left us visitors holding our breath and we tried our best to suppress laughing. The chaps displayed an insensitive confidence with no signs of shyness interfering with their intentions. They made a chat up look like the most casual thing in the world. Some girls, pretty looking and relaxed showed interest in us and we maintained small talk circling round our different worlds of heritage. On the other hand, among us males the dominant topic was painting activities and the odd concern or question about money.

The two Rascals now on their first tour departing from Praha, with the destination being Greece, are rolling by train on a very slim budget with a lot of dependence weighing on help yourself to necessities. Regarding to the history of European Metro painting our two men are on a route passing through cities with virgin Metro systems. Allowing for this situation a lack of security against such activities meets them with every entrance to the underground. Kicking the action off in Budapest they arrived shortly afterwards in Bucharest's *Gare du Nord* to find a layup overwhelmingly open for visitors in afternoons. As well as Sofia's main hanger despite high surrounding walls and watch towers it was also welcoming. If the Rascals came across Metros flanked by platforms you wouldn't have to ask them twice about what's to be done. The pair liked pieces in size, sizes that others wouldn't copy so quickly. Whole-cars and end to ends require time and the nerve to linger and get it done while being trapped in the unexpected. Referring to the region the surprise effect lays totally on their side in case of sudden encounters somewhere in the underground. In those day's there would hardly have been a security guard patrolling or placed permanently on a spot in the Metro maintenance site. In Europe's east for the moment one wouldn't even think of surveillance cameras, movement sensors, automatic light spots, undercover security workers prancing about stations or lurking in parked cars beside the site's outer walls. The Rascals approach on targets was alert and sophisticated to the required degree. Every attempt to get painting done presented the opportunity to experience new situations and allowed them to draw corresponding knowledge for their reaction repertoire. The two being able to fulfil their desires collected affinities and feelings, endured explosions of intensity running from toe up through the stomach to the hairs twitching on their scalps. With every accomplished Metro System, a longing would nearly instantly arise for the next one.

Considering their serious approach to the business quite naturally appeared New York's Metro system flickering through their minds. If they were doing Metro's now and eyeing maps for further destinations, they could surely go straight for the Mount Everest among the many peaks. Sitting in front of a computer and comparing the flight prices and popping into a travel agency for their offer to New York the amount in 2003 figured at 800 euros upwards. Definitely too high in that moment for our motivated Rascals but the time will arrive one day for them to sort out the city's Metro system. So, the two continued to intensify their hobby. Europe, west or east south or north all had cities with Metro systems and for a couple of years the two acted as a team and got their aims done. Mainly by train and with the country connecting Interrail ticket. One day the pair of tracks running parallel to one another began to create separate directions. The Praha Rascal had different intentions to his bratislavian Rascal and unmistakeably the tracks drifted apart. Once more did the Rascal find himself left alone with his cherished occupation. Not alone in the sense of no one to paint with. Through his many tours he had met people who shared similar ambitions and valued what they did. There were equivalents as motivated and committed to the Graffiti action as he was and with them more lay ahead to challenge.

Fortunately for the Rascal and his friend's competition in the sky travel sector increased and through the mediator, Internet, affordable prices emerged to destinations one wouldn't have dreamed of reaching so convenient. The planet was being illustrated as a shop full of exotic offers, just a couple of mouse clicks away. Into the skies, you could fly yourself leaving one continent behind for an attraction on another. The Rascal having been engaged and faithful to Graffiti all along since his youth created for himself an acknowledged reputation which allowed him to transform his hobby into his profession. Accompanying Europe's Graffiti developments its popularity and attention grew firstly through its public position and secondly through the rapid influence of Internet into subjective life.

Individuals and Companies were beginning to discover their taste for the various forms and styles of Graffiti. Street art sprouted up as one creative form of expression and could now with Graffiti be booked and invited to display it's skills in offices, private rooms, public squares and in advertisement for the young and materialistic orientated. Receiving orders for all possible surfaces the Rascal now began to find himself with sufficient cans and money. On the one hand, he maintained his ambition to conquer unvisited Metro systems but pulling on the other arm and hand was time which was now getting fixed with legal painting assignments. Gradually his legal works provided him with sufficient funds to allow him to think realistically of North America.

A flight now in 2014 from a major European Airport cost around 400 euros return. Aware of the vast options North America had to offer, painting wise, friends for such an adventure got contacted and they agreed to grasp the offer and put a road map together.

New York city, the shining star in the dream, was labelled important but he the Rascal wouldn't be able to miss it because it lay in a straight vertical line of major east coast cities bearing the Metro system. All the cities living with a Metro system where going to get visited and done. That was clear and placed equally next to the attempt on

New York.

If you're in the region you might as well go for them all. The bunch of friends made out that the adventure should be achievable within three to four weeks.

Arriving in New York City from further up North the band of painters settled into a hipster dominated Brooklyn borough in the brisk cold season of winter. The Rascal being now where he always wished to be attached his self-being to a vibe that pulsated through the city. He acknowledged the atmosphere as positive and enjoyed the feelings he was experiencing and dealing with while present. Manhattan isolated by water and raging glittering into the air through its tons of cut glass supported by bills of income from exploitation and suppression of people and nature. The Island had to get visited and frequented for presents to take home to Europe.

By the time night fell the place for the main business in town would be selected out of the uncountable choices. A friend of the Rascal from eastern Europe had successfully visited New York a year earlier and shared his experiences with him which helped the Rascal group to set themselves up for the waiting task. The group consisted of seven people and could have easily grown further. The bunch had already enlarged themselves by coincidence. Over social media sites the group discovered that an additional handful of European writers were in town sharing the same ideas. Although one could combine the ideas and easily meet up the common enemy existed and was prowling the Metro depots on an anguishing level. The *Vandal Squad* still operates throughout town combining their force with the regular Police squad.

For a start, the group would have to divide themselves into two smaller groups. Now a days seven people intending to paint a Metro in the city would be strictly careless. Seemingly the counter forces had installed numerous plain cloth officers all over the town including the underground transport ways. Seven people trying to look like a bunch of brand fanatics but moving about long past shop closing time was considered risky. The group divided itself into a quartet and a trio to avoid the otherwise aroused attention. Plus, to diminish the chance of encounters with the squad officers a car was arranged for traveling to the spots of interest.

The Rascal ready for action was keen on winning a wide impression of the city's various types of spots for painting. To begin with their choice fell on the welcoming 111 street elevated layup. When at last the reduced group of writers reached the parked Metro after descending from the stations platform and running along the tracks they had twenty minutes to paint. It's deep in the night and freezing cold. The four of them begin to paint. Astonished by the non-existence of surveillance cameras and further technical support around the layup the Rascal became even more astonished as he looked down between his legs. Underneath them standing at a red light was a cop car. Breathing calmly, he continued painting anticipating they would drive off. Looking down through the logs of wood he again saw a police car. Turning to his friend and telling him of what he saw his friend replied he knew and that's why he won't look down anymore. The group finished their pieces in the intended time and departed happily before the operating Metro arrived in the station of exit. The following night the plan was to visit one of the big outdoor Metro yards. Equipped with the right tools to overcome the double erected fences they set off once more in the depth of the night. Working quietly the group cut their way through the thick fences. In front of them spread out in file were their objects of desire. Looking like they always did beneath the golden orange high beamers. The only change in the Metros appearance was that today's coating gleamed brighter on them than the models of the mid twentieth century.

Sticking to the shade of the carriages the group advanced towards their pointed-out target when suddenly one realized that close to them was a 360-degree camera. Letting no hysteria arise the group of four continued in their direction. To one side of the yard noise cut the nights silence and an operating Metro rushed by with a lengthy swish. Otherwise around them on the premises not a soul was to be seen or heard. No cleaners or drivers or security guards. Arriving at the targeted carriage the first writer in line signalled vigorously with his hand for the others to lay down. The four dropped flat on their stomachs and watched stiffly agonized beneath the carriage how a police car close in distance drove slowly past them on a road below the oversight tower. Lying in the shade the four calmly awaited the polices disappearance. Once gone and back on one's feet the cans came out of the bags and the men began with their colourful pieces. Trying to eclipse the cold temperatures the Rascal steadily finished his piece to his full content and waited till they could collectively take their pictures. Something around a half an hour had passed by and to finish off the action each erased his piece with silver colour completely. Knowing that the police would surely investigate severely into their action it had to be done to minimize the chances of getting found out. Further cities were still scheduled for visits, so it seemed a wise thing to do. The quartet reformed line and left the yard the way they had entered. Feeling positively engaged with the city and the places he visited for painting the Rascal felt the inner calmness of happiness manifesting itself within himself. He liked the city, discovered places he considered beautiful was impressed by the astronomical number of spots for painting but honestly the cost of dwelling in New York was intense.

How nice it would be to come back and share a house with a local. Or return with numbers of fellow writers and work all over town to colour up the metallic cold Metro carriage surface. The Rascal travelling on towards the great lakes embarked a steam boat with wheels big enough to voyage to the west coast and to lands beyond the oceans with un-discovered Metro systems ready for redecorating. The sense of freedom lays within the interest of adventure and self-discovery on the behalf of one's openness and liberty to involve with the surrounding world.

INTENSE PULSATION

*This story gives further depth to the tales in this book
entangling more of surrounding life at its created time.*

As a lad who insisted on knowing his heritage but got taken
away from it for the sake of the family's resettlement into
the homeland of his mother's origin, he had profound difficulties settling into his new environment. Emotional and
sentimental outbursts would erupt in the privacy of the
family apartment as he longed to return to his home and
Irish boyhood.

 The pastures of his childhood had been left behind as
he settled into a four-room apartment with his brother and
sister and both the parents in a small sized block of flats.
Behind the residential estate agricultural land rose lightly
with several farms set in the fields colliding with the forest
which topped off the hills. Out the other side of the flats
window leading down into a small valley the capital city of
the country could be seen distanced beyond fields cut
through by roads.

Comparing the space, he had had on beforehand to roam about and explore, this was certainly different to the wide spread private housing properties and small terraces he now found himself set in between a main crossroad with a gleaming white church above it and easy going side roads leading off it to the housing areas. Earth and trees where now fenced in and forbidden to be trodden upon. A hard comparison to the vast fields with grazing cattle and sheep surrounded by moor ponds little woods and a golf course belonging to a big caravan park occupied mostly by Dubliners in their holidays. The plush green countryside found it's ending above a lowered long stretched strand with the dark green waves of the Irish sea pounding it's beige sand banks which descended into Court town bay.

His mother and father were fairly absorbed during the day with their tasks and duties towards our co-inhabitants who had all sorts of disabilities and (mal)heureusements, fore we lived altogether as a community on the premises of one big estate. Through engaging everyone in the range of their possibilities were we nearly able to cover our life necessities through self-providence.

Once the school bell pierced the loud and noisy air of the break time square centred in the middle of the school building reminding the children to return to the quietness of reciting educational material, you better do as was expected from you. Otherwise the ruling hand would arise with a stick in it threatening to march you off to the school's head master who would then scold the crap out of you whilst chewing on a cold untoasted white toast bread sandwich enriched with a gulp of white tea. The face of the head master would turn red while he roared his fragments of mind at the young boy, one of two in school who wasn't wearing a tie to the uniform, who only got more bewildered seeing the unmistakable warts set upon it bounce along to his rage.

Shut your gob and let me go explore the many developments in my cosmos. "You might want to buy your golf balls back off me later. I'll be down the Balleymoney road just past the Orphan Girl."

The earnings out of the golf ball sale got spent afterwards on the culinary wishes of my brother and sister and the other staff children of housekeeping families of our community.

The neighbouring Orphan Girl Pub fulfilled our wishes for Burgers, chips, drumsticks, gumballs and chewy chocolate bars heartfully. The Orphan Girl is a spacious fine public house supplemented with a take away a disco and a restaurant. These additional offerings tried (where there) to meet the rituals of the thousands of Dublin caravan parkers who would come down to the seaside in there vacant days and months bringing along their loud-mouthed siblings who strayed around just like ourselves. We only ever met their kids on the outskirts of our premises and straight away abuse was hurled at us across the ditch and through the thicket added sometimes by flying sticks and stones but a response never came to short. Otherwise when we were out and about off our premises, we received no special attention and where left alone observing.

The surroundings of our estate where typical countryside Ireland. Wide lush green fields penned in by high thick hedges with red metal barred gates blocking the entrance to the winding narrow road cutting through the countryside. Traffic was scares so one could cycle slightly incautious up and down the lanes. My sister and brother and me where only a year a so apart from one another and the rest of our friends with me being the eldest. I didn't have to often a reason to lead us off our own grounds. Our community had so much space and diversity to offer to us children.

Ten years have passed by and we're in the year 1997 and my parents have decided to bring changes to life which will get approached and attended to on the European continent. Precise in the heart of the western side of Europe in a city at the foot of the Swiss Alps set between various lakes where upon vintage boats sail connecting the coastal towns.

We left Ireland by ferry and travelled by train towards our final destination arriving adventurously in our new region sleeping amidst post mail bags on their night delivery due to some incorrect travel connections. My new community lay just on the outskirts of the city with a couple of fields, industrial zones, housing units and a small forest in between. Our public connection was a private operated regional train, bright orange in colour and it took ten minutes to reach the central station. The ride by bicycle stretched itself over eight kilometres meaning twenty minutes cycling.

Having more or less rapidly learnt the local language and was capable of speaking it authentically, questions summoning my origin where kept firstly at bay. I had my difficulties adopting the dialect but found it quite amusing being able to play with the funny sounding pronunciation of the Swiss German words.

The first bonds I make with same aged boys besides in school are in football clubs I participate with and these lads, two in particular ventured with me into leisure time. The second boy, a lad blessed with an enormous summary of black wavy hair upon his head caught my attention and affection, me calling him cousinly captain skin because he was our teams captain and additionally, I had discovered these folks with shaved scalps.

So probably one day before setting out for football training I told my mother that I wouldn't be straight home afterwards. "What's the reason son", she questioned, "I've got to know this nice fellow, who is in my team and I'll be out with him." I'd asked him once while we were getting dressed in the changing room: "Mate Matry would you mind showing me the town," and he willingly agreed.

Going into town

Me a dark haired, tall slender and sporty or jeans dressed kid, eyes and senses wide open for interesting new situations merrily accompanied him by bus into the city where his neighbourhood lay. It was located just above a clean and slow running river and close to the city centre. The neighbourhood was a well-mixed accumulation of people sharing the tendency to consider alternative ways of handling and living life. Opposite the house where Matry and his sister and parents lived lay beneath the beams of the roof his, his cousins and a neighbouring friend's retreat space. The space consisted of a low main room with two even lower side rooms cramped in beneath the roof. The place was more or less a wreck, the windows were cracked the walls had holes in them and the wooden floor showed it's unaccountable dirty age. The place had funny looking and unfamiliar inhabitants to me who made the residence beside the retreat room appear well fresh and peculiar, in a form that I'd never seen before.

That afternoon an autumn day with the sun lacking it's previous strength I entered the space finding two turn tables centred in the middle room in front of the windows with two descent loudspeakers flanking the table they were lying upon. Set against the walls lay two shallowly cushioned sitting units, on one side an arm chair and on the other side a small sofa. A box was turned over with magazines upon it and here and there lay a plastic bag beholding objects reciting hollow tin metal sounds when moved. Have a seat suggested Matry as he opens up his side bag containing vinyl records taking two of them out and placing them upon the spinners. I sat there wondering what kind of sound was going to come out the speakers while examining the room. Sounds emerged with cuts and scratches in between till a phrase spoken clear and loud amounted: this is the body of the light force, scratch, worse comes to worst my peoples come first spoken on a cool sounding beat and rhythm.

Matry's long musician like fingers pulled gently back the spinning black records and then pushed them with the same delicate handling forwards again. This is true Hip-Hop music he said looking at me with his head bent towards his shoulder clenching an earphone in between. Shortly after we were settling in the door opened and in came a kid with short cut blond hair introducing himself, slightly restrained as Matry's cousin. "I'm Samuel happy to meet you, man of the arch of diversity." Matry's cousin making himself comfortable in the arm chair began slowly to explain what was going on in their retreat room: "What we're listening to is Rap music out of New York." Him, now rapping calls himself Afu-ra. Matry who is getting the music going calls himself Dj Bigfoot, guess why he says and I look down beneath the table already presuming I know why. Here comes KRS One and listen, Jeru the damager is being cut in on the other turn table. Matry also likes to do breakdance. "I like to try myself in rapping and I spit by the name Mc Bonsma." Pointing to the magazines lying on the box in front of us "and together we are a crew which also does Graffiti. Check out the magazines and see for yourself." I feel excited as I hear the definitions new to me ringing through my mind while I reach out for a magazine. Putting back the magazine after wading through the pages acknowledging the, to me appearing bubbly thick letters asking him when they would be going out to do this, hinting with my head towards the pile of magazines.

The kid with the name of the man off the arch, Matry's cousin looks at him and suggests the coming weekend. "Ask your parents if you can stay over at my place on Saturday night" says Matry, his eyes looking over us into the shabby wall, me presuming he's already pondering over the upcoming event. During my adaption to local society my big man, my father isn't coping that well with the same procedures losing his balance upon the path he's taking multiple times to old habits which don't take very well with family life. My parents after a couple of years in Switzerland agree to separation after various salvation attempts leaving me with a tattered world once again. Talking for myself, I can see and understand the reasons for their decision. Momentarily I'm glad my mother lets me sleep over at Matry's which gives me the space and the opportunity to explore our new trinity. Back up in the youth room the two cousins are getting their spray material ready and they explain every necessary object required for the action. Matry will do the crew letters while his cousin's intention is to do a character beside the crew piece. The sketches they've done are included in the events preparation and they look dope to me, a word I've learnt meaning cool. My contribution to the event is to keep a good eye open and servile our surroundings for any human or motorised movement coming our way meaning I'm the lookout. As soon as one of both or even both approach us give us a signal and we move into hiding says Zoah. Right I say and question the place we're going to work. It's not that far from here and at two o'clock in the morning things should be more or less quiet.

Arriving at the spot the cousins go into positions and I place myself opposite them across the narrow road up against a wall. I'm standing stick stiff, eyes fixed on the direction trouble could approach from with my heart beating as if I was up to mischief. Nothing notable occurred while the lads proceeded with their styles upon a low built wall screening off a block of apartments. Zoah stows his cans away in his side bag looks at me with eyes wide open, the work could be finished, and urges Matry to do the same. A couple of seconds later Matry's cans disappear into his bag and he comes over to us smiling beneath his winter cap with his arms open to embrace. Come on lads off we go he says cheerfully and we turn towards the direction we came from. Walking up the dimly lit street, no soul is about except us at this time of night. The road only has residential housing left right along its narrow stretch. During walking I experience a feeling of satisfaction gathering itself inside me.

I ask them if their also satisfied and both respond positive leaving me content with my contribution underlining the feeling produced by our common result.

Through this event my youth was getting nourished by this spraying action and the reception the darkness with its late hours out provoked contained a welcome as well as the opening of a whole new world. The cousins also took me to the legal painting spot, a very long high wall marking the boundary of a rifle shooting range. The place was covered with very nice and expensive pieces and one could wonderfully observe the men and rarely present woman doing their work when out painting. We would take up a less prestigious spot on the wall's length mainly at its end, a space where the other beginners or toys as their called had painted. Their pieces were declared crossable and the backlash if to happen was considered manageable. The duration of these events stressed my patience and on top I seldom had sympathy for the pieces I did. A cool style like most of the other present pieces or like the styles the cousins did, they were talented, just didn't lay in my possibility. My letters looked misshaped and I was always quick to admit it to myself. Back home in the evenings after dinner my exercising time found place and I would retrieve myself to my attic room, put in a rap cd and vigorously draw till I gave up from exhaustion and off to bed I went hoping my sleep would be sufficient for my alarm clocks call in the morning. I didn't want my mother to have to wake me up too much so the questions for her doing so wouldn't arise. School couldn't be dodged.

Graffiti now was definitely forming a second foundation beside my football aspiration and seemingly both didn't harmonize that well together. One day far away from my home and town I was at a tournament with the county's prosperous youth squad which was playing for promotion to higher stages of the sport. Standing as substitute on the side line I suddenly had realization strikes of being on the wrong path. All this manic competition around me I thought and couldn't see myself putting more than my two legs into it although I was a passionate player. So, I decided to quit and relinquished my position for this exciting cross city game with its credible values. Being out in the pulsing city exploring and leaving behind a visible and reviewable mark on its surface had a profounder weight to me than football with its ball orientated triumphs, there was just more to it. One afternoon most likely on a weekend, the three of us where out and about at the wall of fame practising our styles on a base coating of colour. A proper hall of fame production. Multiple colours and unique in styles. Due to my inability of matching the quality that was being performed I insisted on not participating. As time went by the lads were well into their productions, me standing behind them looking upon them and the wall or sometimes nosing about I noticed a slightly older boy, slim in posture, eye'n us from a short distance up the wall. He was tagging around and I recognised him from where I lived. Approaching cautiously, he asked if we also did other things than out here, never the less complementing the work that just had been created. I asked him why did he think so and he pointed out the similarity of letters which he thought he recognised mentioning also a caution warning about some other guys. The other two had now stopped painting and came over to join us. We condemned his presumption all knowing it had to be kept secret and turned to questioning him. The chap was polite, called himself Morris and stood firm bearing confidence related to his experience in the painting game. He stayed the rest of the afternoon with us and he and I shared the journey home. We met up with him more often and of course shortly introduced him to our full effect with the spray cans. Discussions surrounding his entrance to our trinity swiftly arouse and we three came to the happy conclusion of inviting him into our crew. This also meant a new consensus name representing us four had to be created. Settling in to a night of drawing and meddling with the ABC accompanied by a debate over the meaning of the three letters resulted in a common outcome that pleased us all and on top withheld a bit of sense.

Our crew (Dirt on the Stick / D.A.S)

Once the weekend had arrived again little was there to hold us back from getting out at night and executing our crew name. We were all up for spreading it. During the week we would meet up after dinner in our new retreat room, which was different but not better comparing to the old one. It was damp, slightly mouldy and had no windows but it certainly suited us and we quickly made it comfortable for ourselves. Sitting on the sofas and armchairs we would sketch pieces in our black books watch recent Graffiti movies which were quite inspirational, smoke dope to the sounds Matry played for us and discuss our next move. There was also a lot to talk about concerning the Graffiti game. Our city had some 250'000 inhabitants and in half an hour you could cycle from one end of the town to the other. An impressive amount of at least twenty crews shared and selected city surfaces for their purpose at the time which left a lot of work to be done if you wanted to draw acknowledging awareness upon your contribution.

One crew championed in quantity but lacked in style and diversity on the other hand. Another crew championed the other way around. Some specialized on weird remote spots but eventually you would come across their work and others where simply everywhere in town or along the motorway and railway tracks leading into town. We as beginners focused firstly on a decent stylish appearance and then took it gradually direct on to exposed spots. Not to forget mentioning the most remarkable pieces to me were the ones big in size and those flanking the sides of the urban regional trains. On these surfaces you had full colour pieces with all kinds of illustrated fill-ins and backgrounds comparing to the mainly silver or bronze filled in street pieces outlined with black. Enjoying the painted trains Morris and me would meet up on a pleasant summer afternoon and cycle to the nearest railway line where the regional trains circulated and lay in the grass banks leading down to the tracks and admire plentiful running paintings. Back then in the beginning of the millennium nearly every single regional train composition had pieces on its side and would run for several days. The contrast the colours inside the piece's letters made against the blue and white wagons with yellow doors was just amazing. Its existence left a fare impact on me and I was willing and eager to do the same one day. Attempts in doing so in our stadium were considered not very wise because we knew that one chap in particular and other crews where in charge of the places these objects could get painted on. Every now and then I mentioned jokingly the possibility to my crew mates but the fear of retaliation from that tremendous good train painter was to bone shaking. He really had a vicious reputation as to his violent approach on trespassers and we certainly did not want any parts of our bodies harmed or broken.

Meanwhile we were quite satisfied with the proceedings of our new name. Many pieces had been achieved as well as a good amount of tags. Our name was present in many of the towns major streets and we thoroughly enjoyed putting it up out there. Morris and I had done a big chunk of the entire work because our life situations created enough space and time for it. Morris had begun his apprentice as a graphic designer while I was visiting the eve of secondary school. Matry and Zoah visited college added by the situation that their homes weren't designed for nightly getaways. Morris's Mother was regularly out at a boyfriend's leaving the house to himself and I had my attic room where I could tip toe down the creaky wooden stairs at a time no one would hopefully awake in the three-party house and off we went returning an hour or so before day break.

Meeting up in the afternoon with the intention to view our nights production Morris and me were cycling through a neighbourhood of the town on our way to the spot when suddenly the writings on the wall were directed arrow straight towards us as a crew. One is always aware of letters put together on walls or boards as one moves along looking left and right, so we came to a halt in front of this message. "Die DET and DAS, fuck you Toys" written in grey letters on a broad white wall. Both of us were startled and we summoned up a bit of hysteria. What did we do wrong? How come this fierce threat discussed Morris and me directly on the spot and later in comradery between the four of us.

Fear had struck us but none of us could relate to any wrong doings and we strongly rejected surrendering to the nutter of the scripting. The solution to our threatened existence was found in the creation of a new name. Three new letters should solve the problem making the transition difficult to figure out. "DET" the other guy who was included in the threat who we previously had got to know was expelled from gaining any knowledge from us about our transformation. The formation behind the new crew name was a secret which people had to figure out for themselves by which ever clues they could collect. Directly after the foundation we got straight to work. Morris and I launched the first piece in daylight in a remote lake side village next to its train station where we had spent a camping weekend with friends including "DET". Matry and Zoah weren't informed about the action and it was our intention to surprise them as they left the camping ground later than us with "DET". Would he see the piece too when leaving the place for home and would he presume we had done it?

For us as a crew and for me this was a debut in to the game wrapped in suspicion. This intensified the excitement for me because I began to notice that other writers where noticing procedures made by a new crew.

Meanwhile our circle of friends was getting enlarged and one late autumn in 2001 I accompanied a friend from a crew close to us to a mate of his who lived in Berlin who was involved in rap music and Graffiti. This city was a whole new experience and level shown to us by this nice chap who originally was also form our town.

First Berlin had much more Graffiti than I had ever seen in one place. The city appeared to me literally covered in Graffiti, even steep rooftop walls were hit up with pieces and secondly recognizable crew names were everywhere I went. It didn't matter if we moved by foot, bus, circle train or subway, crew pieces flanked the surfaces verifying in height, size and creativity leaving an imposing impression. Special for us two was our prime venture into a seemingly huge intercity train yard full with these white wagons where we did our first pieces on steel surfaces in a light drizzle of rain under very bright flood lights. The experience being new to us and long dreamed of seemed somehow unreal, a kind of haze went through me while I followed the instructions our local friend gave. The outcome was a small colourful piece done with an exciting hand.

Arriving home with all these impressions and vibrant experiences I told my crew mates we should do the same as the Berlin crews, expand all over the city except for the trains. We could go out every night, each coming weekend and create a remaining impression.

For me I was determined to see through my intentions as good as the other life circumstances would allow me to. To accompany me I found an equal motivated and determined partner, my mate from the crew friendly to us who I had accompanied to Berlin. We met up to three times a week at hours past midnight and focused on spots along every bus line. Those night outings meant a lot to me creating feelings of self-confidence with dependable senses of being someone and something. The parts of earth we moved about on and decorated in the quiet and deserted hours of the night which one without reason wouldn't be able to experience and be able to acknowledge its existing beauty. To me it's the co-observation of silence spreading after departed noises, racing clouds in the moons silky light, the appearance the night gives to urban and country-side objects that enrich your senses while out and about. Ones self-being poised listening for the respond of safety or danger to one's presence. The various physical modes you switch your body and mind into when handling the existing situation and reacting to sudden developments turning into existence in a blink of an eye or through the shout of a human, the scratch of an animal or the echoing of a horn or siren. Over a couple of months of intense work our progress could be measured in both quality and quantity. All of us four had participated the best his possibilities had allowed him to. Every effort done by us as a group or in a pair or done alone got warm and kindly celebrated. It felt nice and good being able to dedicate one's energy in a passionate way to a cause created through comradery. We were a team and every individual was his own unit with valuable qualities which enriched the whole.

Each of our presences embedded in our cosy warm retreat room on sofas and armchairs with a wide range of music, books, Graffiti movies and Graffiti magazines added by sheets of clean paper and markers for drawing created a harmonic familiar feeling and surrounding which I cherished. We were a group of adventurers exploring society's offerings meeting one another's intentions. At the age of 14, 15 and 16 we flew to Amsterdam together to experience more self-determination. Painting activities got set equal with smoking skunk so far, we were allowed to enter a coffee shop and we curiously set out for both. I had earned previously my first couple of hundred Swiss francs cleaning a school building during spring holidays so money was on hand. The cousins had family outside town to visit and while I and Morris stayed back in town, we bumped into a pro Palestine demonstration which ended in riots with charging policemen wielding long rubber sticks on horseback with chaos spreading over the Dam square which created a lot of excitement with in me.

Experiences were getting intense and wild both home and abroad but they didn't create any aversions within me. More so the opposite was gaining support and I seldom had to think twice about what I was doing. Even after getting caught twice at home red handed for painting in the early hours of the morning by a private security man who held us captive till the police came couldn't turn my intentions and affections for the thrills and adventures around. I told my mother that I just wouldn't get caught anymore and that it was only colour that was bringing trouble. The consequences for my actions ended up in me scrubbing off the tags I had placed on the posh Auto-garage in broad daylight which did feel a bit humiliating. Back on the track after meetings with a juvenile judiciary who understood the value of second chances, we discussed in the circle of friends the necessity to handle our actions with more caution and care. Morris and Matry had shared the experiences with me and we didn't want them to be repeated. We came to the conclusion that we had to watch out better while painting and afterwards when finished we would either hide the used cans or at least carry them in a way that one could throw them away immediately if a police car showed up anywhere near us. It could regularly happen that they would stop next to us or just roll slowly besides us and ask what we were up to. Policemen on night patrol would commonly look out for young people moving about at such a late hour and it was also wise to have a reasonable answer ready in response to the question for why one was out so late.

Being out in the depths of the night and engaged in physically tiring activities didn't support my appearance and engagement in school. I hardly shared my night activities with anyone of my class. It felt better to keep them to myself because I didn't want any of them asking if they could join in. Due to my tiredness and thoughts of where and what to paint next followed by how it was going to get done left me mainly incapable of receiving the whole summary of the subject that was being thought in front of me. I didn't have an aversion for school it was just my concentration capability was quickly narrowed and it couldn't sustain itself and I regularly ended up sitting outside the classroom. Practical handcraft lessons and outdoor activities where more my case. On entering ninth grade the subject apprenticeship and college accompanied the entire school year and to me it was clear that my concentration and scholarly efforts wouldn't match the requirements a college expected let alone me making it to the end of the ninth year. Occasionally I found myself cursing the question which led to the decision wanted from me about my close future. Painting meant and was to me what I liked to do and otherwise I hadn't any dreams of a profession. Who the heck is asking this decision off me anyway came often to my mind, with me realizing in the end that it's meant to bring financial survival. Well then that's quite and Outlook I have to create for myself.

Graffiti was prior to me but I was aware that it wouldn't bear money in the next couple of years so some apprenticeship had to be found none the less. Sitting and discussing my affinities with a professional advisor and coach we settled on the professions of the mailman, the landscape gardener and the chef de cuisine. Each of the three professions contained an element in which I could share a common base, a healthy foundation for me to visualize a development that would suit me. The main element of interest to me behind the postman and the landscape gardener was clearly the value of being outside and engaged in practical labour. What supported the chef the cuisine decision I can't clearly recall. I had been kicked out of cooking class in school but maybe the prospect of being able to travel with that craftsmanship had been sufficiently persuasive.

Teen-aging

Upon the horizon of my personal future loomed the education and capability prospects of the world and my engagement with it. My first preference is still my Graffiti commitment. And my first most wish an engagement on train compositions with me and my friends painting their flanks with the finished work traveling through our region finding its termination in Graffiti magazines, especially in our own local one. This prospect of mine included expansions to my otherwise solid enthusiasm. Further ahead upon my horizon circled an additional sense of brightness, agility combinable with a world of opportunities, chances and possibilities. The main combinable importance resulted in possessing a certificate of profession which would help put bread and vegetables on my plate. As for more, who knows for certain what will be, thought I who knew where he'd come from but didn't want to fix a sole destination for the cause of variation in shows. The unfolding of many worlds some withholding harsh and incomprehensible sides to life which myself took a part in receiving and in distributing a share combined with the co-existence of charity, goodwill, love and human kindness dominated my sense and relation to joy and inner warmth. After sniffling labour praxis and the air surrounding each profession, my choice fell upon the atmosphere stimulating my mood on all levels and it had to be the kitchen. In the place I had visited lay such a buzz of bubbling tension in the air accompanied with humour and vividness, it just felt like the place wright for me. The master of the kitchen a man confident of his skills and a shouting head on top of himself offered me the place as an apprentice without hesitation. Luckily my oven for baking wasn't in his kitchen rein. Mine lay in another kitchen belonging to the same private hospital group. My master and chef was a French man with a nervous foot followed by an equal Swiss man both steadily concerned about ones progress and development and luckily both never relieved their orders in a state of shouting. The cuisines culinary style was traditional French and got prepared by a broad team of skilful and demanding Swiss chefs and servicemen from Sri Lanka.

In the meantime, beside the adjustments I was directing towards my labour participation outlook the expansion of our crew name received support from my strong will to maintain progress in the development of my Graffiti style. Through our work amidst the city's form people from the Graff scene had took notice of our engagement on a positive note. Our styles where diverse appeared fresh and we had met the challenge difficult spots would demand off one's devotion. In these times we were also well aware of the other crews doing their thing and where a number of them would meet and hang out together. The spot was an old riding school fortress hosting an autonomous alternative youth centre with a twilight reputation among the county's citizens. The place as it is, still enjoys fame throughout the nation for its battled erection by many a town citizen in the 1980's and the ongoing till today disputes with the city council and its authorities.

The riding school as it is called till today had much to offer to young men like ourselves. A sense of anarchy hung in the air with its fragrance assembling people of various cultural directions seeking a peaceful and tolerant ground to tangle one's spirit of interest. It is a true melting pot shared by a conscious crowd of political activists and debaters plus open-minded art creators and individuals living on the edge of society. The building by size is precise a complex providing much space which is inhabited by cultural stages such as theatre, cinema, concert halls a restaurant a bar an information room and a print studio plus rooms for same sex comfort and tolerance. Occasionally the four of us and other friends would hang out in the bar dancing to Hip Hop or chill outside on the piazza in mellow evenings observing life and the sometimes-obscure scenes. At night time beneath the railway bridge stemmed by concrete pillars which also got used as an illegal hall of fame junkies in reckonable numbers would nourish their addiction by sticking openly their needles into veins you would never consider using. Suddenly a fierce fight could break out among thieves and drug dealers or between intoxicated individuals and we would be standing there with jaws wide open. Among the tense of people, you could also spot guys tagging around or occasionally doing a piece on the riding school or beneath the bridge. The building was anyhow covered in Graffiti verifying from political slogans to classic Graffiti.

The guys doing the tags and pieces revealed themselves to the onlooker but only a few took proper notice of their actions which also included them pointing and nodding towards the pieces passing by on the trains above us.

One mid-week evening while passing time with my partner in action outside the bar of the riding school before setting off for painting he greeted a chap. I recognized him as a fellow close to the train painters and my mate introduced me to him. He was maybe four years older than me and was tall and slim built with nearly a shaved dark-haired head. His eyes closely examined me and straight away he questioned my involvement with Graffiti. My response didn't give my membership directly away and I said he would find it out sooner or later anyway. (It could also happen that someone would come up from behind and fumble the bottom of your backpack checking to see if he's assumption for you being a writer and you carrying cans was wright.) A couple of weeks later after the chap in the meantime had approached me once again in the riding school full of compliments for our work, he then invited us to paint with him and his crew. Matry and me met up with him who belonged to one of the towns major crews and we did some action together. This chap and his friends were painting on a much riskier scale than ourselves and appeared to be moderate punks which I found impressing and refreshingly exciting. After experiencing some time together, I realized that a new level of Graffiti was being approached.

The guys from this crew were quite fond of our work and besides being asked if we would like to join their crew I was asked if I would like to handover some photos for the local Graff magazine *Nonstop*. The four of us were delighted with the proposal and I felt our efforts were leading to material outcomes. Back in our retreat room we discussed the transition and sorted the photos we had of our work and made a selection of the ones we thought were the best and suitable for our presentation. At the end of our talks the conclusion was that we would favour to remain independent as a crew. We were content and happy as things were. Unfortunately, we hadn't considered to make copies of the distributed photos and were double disappointed when we collected a fresh print of the new magazine to sadly discover that near to nothing had been printed and on top after my insistence that the original photos had got lost after the final selection for the magazine was finished. Together we felt the disappointment of the loss and the non-publishing. On we go lads was our collective response to the pitiful set back. Following our introduction to this highly active crew their support and involvement for us began to engage us with others from the local Graff scene which brought more introductions. Meeting these people during the week at the spot late in the evening before everyone would spread out to paint, we would chat about our actions, make jokes over circling joints and get to know each other time after time better. All the lads where a least two years older than myself which didn't matter to me but I realised that I shouldn't ask too many unnecessary questions and especially act with a certain aura of confidence. Holding my tongue was a bigger challenge for me because the elder didn't like it too much when the young chap spoke free and direct. Appearing confident was an easier case due to my relation to our work and you had enough examples who appeared to be confident. Among these new figures was a crew who concentrated fully on painting freight wagons and trains parked in remote areas so they wouldn't interfere with the core of train writing.

After various encounters I became friendly with two from that crew and one evening after me showing an interest for their work and actions was asked if I would like to join them for some action on a scrap train. Joy mounted within me and I was happy and felt lucky that I was heading for the steel surfaces. On a week night we met up and drove to the spot which lay beneath the foot of a pyramid shaped mountain embedded in the alpine region. The available train was an old model waiting to get scrapped due to the new models that were being inserted into the transport systems new fleet. Besides my joy for being allowed to discover the world of train painting, the thought of not being able to take my whole crew along with me stressed. There were no invitations for them to join in and I didn't want to risk getting expelled due to the lack of space and place for us all. (But later on, a new visit to Amsterdam when meeting up with a guy I had got to know who painted trains in Holland, I arranged a meeting with him for my crew mates and other friends who had joined in on the trip to go and paint Dutch *bananas* while enjoying the country's capital.) A feeling of guiltiness which I wasn't quite sure if I was or not tickled me every now and then because I felt I was acting selfishly in not insisting if all my mates could join in painting trains at home.

My crew mates didn't make a big issue out of my procedures and I didn't feel like asking if my sole actions concerned them. I didn't know where things were going and how the outcome of my actions would be except that I wanted to do them good. Although I was leaving familiar grounds for occasional new ones, I kept close to mind that through my actions there would and should be opportunities in the future for us to paint trains together.

After my first local train our meetings became more frequent and through these, I got to know more people mainly sharing the same leisure interest. Among these young adults were also some prominent figures out of the steel Graff scene. These chaps were a lively and communicative group of men in their twenties always tagging around and sharing joints among one another. Being around them intensified my excitement and I felt I was finding the place I was looking for.

Due to their intense devotion and attitude towards painting one could meet them nearly every day in the afternoon at the spot relaxing and enjoying their pieces passing by upon the railway bridge from the stooled front terrace of the riding school.

Sitting around a table with the younger guys in the bar of the riding school chatting about past and future actions the creator of the local Graff magazine joined our circle mentioning that he had a special job for us if we wanted. A fair amount of copies from the new edition were destined for Madrid and we could deliver them if we saw any pleasure in doing so. In his description of the job he supplemented the task with the possibility of being able to paint Spanish regional trains as well as the Madrid Metro. Now that was music in our ears and we agreed it would definitely be a great pleasure. Seeing that the painting level would possibly get raised again I got to thinking during school lessons of how this adventure could get turned into reality. The first pillar required for such an event was at hand and lay close ahead in the form of time. The second pillar consisted of money which with us being six wouldn't need to big a share pro person and all we needed was petrol, cans and food. It still required all of my monthly pocket money an amount of 250 francs which was meant for everything I needed in my private time. The third pillar consisted mobility which could be provided to us by my father who had a hyper small mini bus and he didn't need it on a daily basis. Most important though was to have the foundation meaning the voyage to be allowed. These components seemed reasonable to me and after reflecting and juggling them back and forth I first engaged the lads before revealing my thoughts to my mother and father. My reflections were combined with the fact that I had summer holidays coming up which marked the closure of my ground school attendance such as the preparation time for my apprenticeship. My demands had legitimacy I thought but accompanying them hovered also the feverish sound of adventure which I wasn't too sure my parents would agree to. Unsure of their answer I explained my intentions in detail to them surrounding the trip, except the painting part and semi surprised because the change of allowance did exist, they granted me my wish.

The tiny Mini-Bus

The mini-bus was a slim tin-plate Bordeaux red build and had no extra or additional space than necessary. Six of us filled the seven-slim measured sitting places accompanied by our minimized luggage plus the odd 150 magazines got tucked in around us on the floor and behind us in the slim booth.

The magazines piled up on each other collectively weighed heavy and were placed on the left inner wall of the booth. On the evening before our departure one of us six had gotten his hair cut and unfortunately the outcome was close to a bald head. Sitting together in the living-room of their shared apartment we all found the new look amusing and through the laughter we all agreed to a unite look so the rest of the hair upon our heads came tumbling down. Without our caps on we probably looked like a wright bunch of eggheads. Never-mind I thought unable to grasp a clear vision of what lay ahead of us. Go with the flow and don't risk a lip to often because I was eight years younger than the oldest of the us and he had the say over the group and operated on a short fuse. He was anyway the king of the Graff scene, and the fierce chap who had threaten us with harm but now we were venturing on to friendship.

Off we went with French rap music blaring out of a portable tape player because the mini-buses one was broke, down the motorway in modest speed towards the route of the sun, crossing through the south of France in the direction of Catalonia. Our circle had two drivers, so we were capable of making lengthy stretches at a time. This was a bit unpleasant and nerve wrecking for us in the back of the hot car which sweltered under the strong southern sun as we drove along a the strongly trafficked *route de soleil*. Easing the situation, we discovered that we could lower the lean of the middle bench, so we could lie and straighten our otherwise cramped legs out across the whole back part of the car like on a double bed. Above us for the extra feeling of liberty one could slide open a hatch in the roof bringing in gushes of fresh and cooling air. The hatch also gave a watch tower position. It was nice being able to stand upright in the centre of the bus feeling the cool air pushing against my chest challenging my stand of ground while I gazed at the dry sunburnt Spanish hills reaching into the distance or out over the impressive vast strange looking dessert planes dotted with rocks on our way to Madrid. Two days have passed with us sleeping outside in the grass at motorway rest places. Through the dessert we moved allowing once the oldest chap on his plea to try out his driving skills after he eventually got the clutch right in an exciting driver exchange situation at a toll barrier while the police were overlooking the traffic. Once in Madrid our contact guided us to a camping site outside the city where we erected only one tent because it seemed utterly crazy to go into a plastic hut in breath taking 40 degrees by night.

Gathered between the car and tent we sat smoking and talking, I had begun to smoke due to the give-away prices for cigarettes in Romania. Before going on the trip, I had spent the end of my school time on a class work engagement for a local school in Romania added with cultural outings. Our camp was in a small rural countryside town settled on the banks of a sparkling river predestined for swimming during the hot summer days. Our school was in partnership with a Waldorf school institution and it was schedule that we offered them our support as a last experience in the tenth school year. Unfortunately, we ran early out of labour but on the other hand we had more time to entertain ourselves which was accompanied by getting to know cigarettes. The price per packet was about one Swiss franc. Before leaving for Romania I now naturally wondered if there would be a chance for painting trains, so I asked an older school mate and close friend if the possibility existed. He told me on my questioning at home that there did exist a close train yard, so I had planned to try out my train painting luck for sole experience. Deep in the night I slipped off and tip toed over train tracks past quiet farm houses standing dark beside the tracks in the delta plane for at least half an hour turning off the line at a junction which lead to the yard but on arrival discovered that the place was full of stray dogs. After nosing about delicately on the main grounds I decided to return home unsuccessful because of the dogs appearing behind every corner of the otherwise plentiful filled train yard. It was very quiet and a dog howling off at one's appearance would ruin the situation. It was exciting and daring but I didn't feel like pushing the too me unknown Romanian ways, let alone a chunk of flesh missing out of my leg.

Back in Madrid the local man who had awaited us gathering the magazines inquired if we were also interested in painting. We vigorously nodded and the oldest of us exchanged a mobile-phone number for a meeting later on that night. What did they have for painting: regional trains, inter-city trains, high speed trains and the prestigious white with blue side stripes metro train? Sitting there and more or less listening I observed that six of us were probably a bit too many to join in the fun. The phone call with the invitation came and the oldest decided who would go along. Four of us had to stay behind and hope that the Madrilenian painters were highly motivated and willing to take us on further actions.

In the middle of the sticky hot night our mates returned with their action unfinished and unfortunately one chap with half a finger missing. His finger ring had got caught on the prick of barbed wire after he dismounted a fence pulling his finger apart. Thankfully the hospital took care of his wound because what came afterwards needed a decent bandage.

We're at our next meeting point somewhere in this to me overwhelmingly large city just after lunch time the night after the accident and are welcomed by a euphoric, dynamic young madrilène man in sportive shorts with a simple sports brand t-shirt wearing runners. He's accompanied by four Portuguese lads who are literally the same age as us and also sportively dressed. One of them seemingly the communicative leader is exactly my age, six-teen. Our introduction is heartful and warm and we exchange our backgrounds. We've parked in an urban area outside a Metro station and Zant, the madrilène explains what's going to happen. His confidence supported his description of the event so truthful that a response opposing him would alienate yourself and I don't think we understood much he said anyway.

The Metro

Standing together in a baking metro wagon lightly occupied, traveling along a stretch of tracks set outside in an open city space Zant indicates to us to wait where we are and walks off to the driver's cabin reverse our traveling direction and opens the cabins door with a key. A minute later he waves at us to follow him and before he brings the Metro to a halt informs the passengers kindly over the microphone what's about to occur. He mentioned something about tourists. Oh my god I think, move, just follow the others who are climbing out of the cabin through the driver's side door down onto the tracks. The sun is scorching and Zant declares the action for on. Go, go, andele andele, come on come on he yells in his Spanish tongue pointing to the long stretch of white metro wagons in front of us standing still in the middle of the line beneath a clear blue sky. As we move upon the small rocks along the wagons, we rapidly organize ourselves each pulling out of his bag a can and hastily each begins to paint. The style I'm now doing has been developed on beforehand and is a simple single letter with small ones placed inside at the bottom of its bulk. The style has come just in the right moment to fulfil its purpose and is easy to accomplish in the assumingly short time we have to get finished. Moving from left to right on my tipped toes so I could reach the wished height, filling up the letter widely with silver, a quick glance along the side of metro seeing the other eight moving in the same manner accelerated my excitement to a level that felt (undeclarable) undeletable good. Honestly, I didn't really know what was going on except that we were painting but afterwards on the other side of the fence we climbed over shortly before the driver retook control over the metro and continued its journey, we all gleamed and grinned at each other bewildered and sensually in ecstasy. The local guy acted and talked as if this was the general way to handle painting business here in Madrid and he encouraged us to act freely. People wouldn't take notice of spray painters he said. Just look out for the police. Later on, in the night we met up with him and ten other local guys to attend another mission. Meanwhile during the afternoon, we did as he said and had painted freely upon road bridge walls, road walls and other sorts of walls. First a bit shy but as no one reacted to our behaviour except for horning motorists all boundaries broke loose. It felt remarkably good and relieving, like Switzerland belonged to another planet and we had just discovered a new planet with vigorous air.

Night had drawn in and we found ourselves, a large lively group of young men above a handed opened emergency shaft looking down a concrete hole with a ladder attached to its side. Down we climbed entering an abandon dark station from behind a door which we passed descending down onto the open metro tracks of a round scarcely lit tunnel. Walking for a couple of minutes the tracks brought us to a parked Metro composition.

Traffic was obviously over I thought as I took up my place in between the sixteen of us next to Jones who was painting next to another sixteen-year-old who looked more like a twelve-year-old. Altogether we painted the entire length of the composition, every single available surface including the front. In half an hour we were finished and had to retreat hastily, the air was very sticky, back up through the hatch bumping into security officers sitting in their car overlooking the hatch helpless. As we moved on passing by them, we couldn't suppress laughing and waving at them.

Our stay in Madrid continued in such fashion and manner even reaching more intense and mental moments where luck must have been on our side.

Summarizing the adventure, the thrill and attitude these guys created in this urban environment was breath taking and enhancing. The city appeared to me as one big playground with plenty of installations withholding fun and adventure for you and your friends. Everything we were doing occurred to be alright, nothing was getting seriously damaged or harmed and the paths and doors we were using to reach the wished outcome lay there in existence. The madridlen guys just had the keys and recipes to unlock their additional potential and we were lucky to meet them.

Yes, the experiences and displays of human control and agility left a deep impact on me as I considered their behaviour and stories while traveling home to my dwelling and plate of taste. Our town didn't have a subway unfortunately but we had trains on the other hand floated through my thoughts sustaining a part of my existing fantasies which suited my ideas of possible actions but didn't fully satisfy my frankness for the exceptional. What had happened back there with me in the past seemed uncommon and not part of the community I was living in. This metro painting game opened a field of actions and hospitality with its vast and distanced sites and people spread out in a region of the world. I inherited the developable approach to reach out to them and achieve goals that matched my perception of a worthwhile existence. These bunch of men accompanied seldom by women had sketched a sense of independent life valuable to the grand interference of dogmatic money. I didn't have much at the time, my friends didn't have much of it but we found ways of having an exceptional time despite that shared by many fact. And besides the forbidding shields it felt correct to acclaim the creatable experiences lying ahead in existing spaces you had to dare enter and engage with.

We are on our home journey and two of our group have left the mini-bus in Barcelona. The rest of us enjoyed an active time in the coastal city and are now charging up a mountain on the French motorway in the frontier region to Switzerland when all of a sudden our mini-bus begins to loose pace till it can't accelerate to more than 10 km/h. Lucky for us we've just made it to the top of the mountain and stop on the emergency lane to give the vehicle a moment of rest. A couple of minutes later a motorway assistance worker appears in a car and offers us his aid. "Not to worry good man," we reply, "it's going downwards from here on so we'll be alright." The lack of money and the belief in good fortune motivate our answer. On jumps the engine, a relieving good sign and we continue slightly nervous our ride and thanks to the steepness we reach 80 km/h. Arriving at the bottom of the hill the Swiss boarder awaits us, and we gladly pass through in the required foot speed. From there onwards the mini- bus didn't go over 40 km/h and we were forced to use the emergency lane when possible causing otherwise short traffic jams on road work sites. Finding the last bit of the journey rather funny and typical for the whole two-week holiday we arrived by night never the less at my mate's home taking six hours longer than usual from the boarder. Once the car got turned off it wouldn't jump on again and we had to tow it to my fathers who calmly accepted the situation as it came home mentioning we should have left it behind to burn, except for the number plates. Later on, the mechanic who inspected the car for its dysfunction discovered a crack on the axle of the back wheels where the heavy load of magazines had been placed. My father inquired of course how things had gone and I really was only able to reply with "quite adventurous and we did a bit of painting." The crack in the axle silently interpreted the weight of occasions we were led into in Madrid but I couldn't summon up the courage to go into detail because the experiences appeared to be too crazy. Death would have had a couple of opportunities to interfere with our actions, maybe then when we entered a metro wagon from (down on) the tracks below the platform, up over the cables connecting the wagons. In through the small door between the carriages we scrambled, 15 of us while the Metro began to accelerate. Each pushed each other so everyone getting in could survive and shake of the security guards who were following us and getting in our way while we tried to get to a station further up the line to recapture photographically our previous done pieces. It was half passed six in the morning.

Apprentice (Chef de cuisine)
Half an hour later at seven o'clock began my second serious occupation. Piles of salad heads verifying in sorts, vegetables in different sizes, shapes and colours were ordered for our patients and lay ready to be processed on the shiny chrome surface of the greens manufacturing section. My first teacher in the kitchen Mr Selatamby who was kind and patience with me and chef of this section was now responsible to show me how to handle, peel and shape the goods into its demanded form. During my tasks, like peeling fifty kilos of potatoes after they popped out of a pre-peeling machine, my thoughts would easily sway off to the depths of Europe's capitals, considering when and with whom an action could get fulfilled.

The Madrid holiday had forged us six lads together and we nearly all shared the same aspirations. Visit cities that had a Metro system and paint it as effectively as possible. At first, we looked around in our own circle of friends if anyone of us had a friend living in such a city who might be able to create the first steps to our prolonging's. Then slowly after gaining some experience of our own we set out to achieve our own idea and plan of painting that self-discovered parked Metro.

How nice it was to arrive at a Metro end station for example in a Milan suburb and discover after tracing the direction of the line lying below the ground that the plot of earth you came across close to an old building, temporarily provided an entrance over a scaffold down through the emergency shaft into the tunnel, where spot on, a Metro was left to rest overnight. As soon as the driver left after parking it there, we tip toed quietly out of our hiding place and banged the wagon with our letters from top to bottom in shiny silver. A nice additional discovery later on was the effect the runners possessed Mark was wearing when I took a picture of him posing in front of the spread-out piece behind.

Upon the picture you saw him leaning slightly backwards in the industrial scenery with his shoes shinning like flashlights because the outer shell of his shoes were made of reflectable material and this enriched the picture.

Every single vacant moment longer than three days from work got turned into an outing out across the country's boarder. If shorter we remained in our region and painted local trains or town walls.

Euro Inter-rail

The new development this hobby was unleashing within me began to summon up an intense devotion which I considered unfit for sharing at home let alone at work. For the sake of my apprenticeship and the peace in our family household, I kept it near to an inexistent secret. Seldom did my mother question my where being because I always returned safe and sound home and turned up at work on time even if it meant swapping the train for the bicycle.

When I was obliged to comment, then as gentle as possible accompanied with a secure and steady expression touched with confidence which was the truth or later would turn into the truth. None of us would even speak about getting caught. The possibility was naturally there but at one stage we found out it was best not to talk about getting caught at all or any other unlucky scenarios. The proceedings of the actions would undergo a serious discussion on beforehand combining all possible scenarios that could occur out of the existing structure of actors. We all enjoyed and cherished our lives, so we always reminded each other of the multiple dangers emerging while moving along, especially keeping the remembrance alight in ones conscious of the third electrified rail.

One did occasionally pick up nasty stories on the journeys, but they had sorely happened, and none should lay ahead of ones or the others missions.

Life was a wonderful endurance of many a day and month in general when out and about in the cities with the lads or at home in the summer months when swimming in the pure river, enjoying the vivid company of one's close friends and messing around with booze supplemented by dance music. The spirit that surrounded me felt comfortable and obviously a female onlooker, who gleamed reversible through her catchy eyes and from the elegance of her slim stretched tall body placing glances of attraction with the resulting attention drawing me to her, entangling us into a sensual whole. And this in the archway of the grand wooden door of the ridding school.

The feelings we created together in those first weeks of our connection to one another evoked an unknown to me hunger for sensual reception and the returnable pleasure of providing it. Her loving and gentle appearance set beneath light chestnut hair which I adored invited me to spend a sort of time valuable beyond everything else existing to me, lured me away from adventures we had begun on our first Inter-rail to the east of Europe. It felt like I had found myself and I wanted to caress myself around her more than achieve points in the big boy's game. Off I went towards Switzerland with a swelling heart which thumped and ached even more as the train sped through the marvellous lush green mountaineer valleys of the Austrian Alps leaving my mates and Budapest behind. The choice I had made to desert the company of my friends followed an inner urge. They understood my decision and maybe the painting success we had enjoyed loosened the thrive for achievements among us all.

To give a glimpse of the picture back there in Budapest, we have succeeded in painting an Austrian intercity train plus directly afterwards moved over to an ocean blue Hungarian regional train standing aside the Austrian one but reversed so we had enough space to take photos of our pieces. The temperature in this late hour of night was intense and humid, seemingly typical for this part of Europe in the summer months. Cheerfully we relieved ourselves of our t-shirts and painted just in our shorts and runners. The trains where located next to Budapest central station behind a red brick wall roughly two meters high, set there to keep us and others at bay. Not being able to see beyond the wall brought up concerns. Were there workers or security guards inside we wondered but we would only know once we had landed on the other side. Determined to prove ourselves and without further options, except street painting, we pulled ourselves each next to another up on top of the wall with cars passing next to us on a wide street. After climbing over we found a big iron pipe going along the inside of the wall to stand on. We've got to chance it, meet the fall to the ground below hanging from the pipe. Landing stable on our feet we paused for five minutes in a shaded spot looking and listening for movements around us. To our left in the blue train parked aside the white and red Austrian one is a cleaning squad hurling full black plastic bags from where their standing out of the trains side door obviously finishing off their task. We wait till we hear their voices die away in the heat as they head towards buildings in the direction of the station. Total quietness regains its space among the rows of trains, roofs shimmering copperish from the orange lights high above. Looking at our object of desire we divide up the space available upon the wagons and command ourselves to get started.

Waking up earlier than wished the next morning molested by the feverish heat, which didn't retrieve in the hours of dawn, we snatched a nice spinach sheep cheese pastry snack from a bakery outside our hostel and headed for the Metro. No one had any objections to why we shouldn't try our luck on the Metro, it was more so an expectation that we all agreed too. A friendly rascal while visiting Bratislava had told us about a suitable spot for daytime action on one of the Metro lines end stations. "It's easy," he said, "use the tree next to the wall to climb over and you've got five minutes to paint upon the platform while the driver walks to the other end of the Metro."

We're sitting in the dark blue metro, a vintage model of soviet manufacture. The air below the surface is thick and hotter than outside, close to unbearable really as sweat arises upon one's forehead and dribbles down the spin also when seated. We agree over puffing and fanning ourselves with maps and occasionally one pokes his faces up to the draftee window that the described plan sounds feasible.

Arriving at the appointed end station we descend individually in the dense flow of passengers mount the escalator arising from the outdoor platform. It's the same platform we're meant to paint upon but only that we're at its distanced other end. The escalator takes us to the heart of the station spread out on a Passover above the platforms. Many people are minding their business's in small shops and on cardboard stalls erected throughout the passageway offering a vast range of items and products such as cheap clothes, cleaning utensils, handyman objects, fresh cooked handmade food and many piles of journals and magazines. A peasantry spirit surrounds the people going about their way in this tube of a Passover. The journey has taken us nearly an hour to get here and we're feeling dehydrated and already exhausted. We buy some water, stand still in front of a stall in search of the exit in the direction we suppose we have to go. Overlooking the moving heads around us we hope that the present guards standing with their backs pressed against the wall didn't take us for painting tourists if they've noticed us at all. Two of us are stale white and blonde but otherwise we match the common fashion. Simple colourful summer clothing. Once outside the station a forest consisting of birch trees, European alder and beech trees erupts beyond a wide tarmacked parking space occupied with cars and mini vans in front of us with the described road leading into it along the outer wall of the station. People leaving the station like us are walking into the forest, so we agree there must be a path parallel to the road which is surely better to use than walking along the busy road drawing on attention. After a couple of minutes of walking the path becomes slender and disperses into many thin ones leading off to the left and right twirling into the thicket. Surprisingly scattered around in the bushes and below the trees, people are lying curled up or stretched out sleeping. Heaps of shit covered by tissues freckle the path we take leading proximately towards the road and wall we've been told of. Yes, we're here where we're supposed to be. Opposite us across the road we can see the roof of an arriving Metro beyond a wall covered with tags (GLK & RCLS) we recognise from magazines and movies. We agree that this must be the place.

Now we have to find a gap between the four lanes of traffic which occurs rarely but after while we finally make it across in a scurry. The wall is rather high and attached to it are two lines of barbed wire. Close to the wall stands a young tree with one branch going out over the wall. We pull ourselves up to the height of our gins gaining enough view necessary to overlook the situation below. The metro arrives at the platform. The driver packs his bag descends from his cabin and walks aside the compositions to the other head. This procedure takes roughly four minutes. Between us, the wall we have to climb over, the space leading onto the platform which we also have to mount by pulling ourselves onto doesn't match the idea of our capabilities considering the four minutes available for accomplishing. Not to mention the possibility of getting seen when on the platform and then where are we going to go with havoc bound to arise, the station with those mutual murky masculine guards or into the depths of this outlandish forest? Oh yes and boys our backpacks are kind of in the way just like the traffic. Reality appears to be cruel and the effort to succeed within too risky so comradely we agree to return and leave the situation to others.

As the train I'm sitting in when leaving Budapest passes the spot where we had painted the previous night in central station, I can see close by the spot a dog pound with a several black beasts prowling their cage.

Once at home I headed straight to her house believing that the early morning time is more than inviting for a surprise appearance into the warmth of her adolescent chamber. To me such a performable option meant stirring myself back to an observant haven willing to offer me space and safety for my intimacy.

The fuse had been touched by the ignition once again and my ambition for painting sparked to a flame willing to spread to a fire containing recognition the size of its competitors. One could count on stories of achievement and adventure throughout Europe which therefore could grant you a further story and experience with individuals or crews that followed a style or knowledge of execution suitable to be integrated into one's own summary.

These were the undertakings I cherished the most. Departing the routines of daily life and local bound development, sitting in your comfortable train seat with a definite adventure and encounters lying on mind and in the distance ahead of you. It was gratitude and realization of being able to mount or overcome the so-called boarders written on shields, either in company of an equal eager friend or in the solitude of one's own sanity. The target now was primarily a Metro model then all the city's different line models following the modest option of a regular train or an urban street piece. Additionally, I set myself the task of verifying each piece style the best I could. Creativity withheld the result and reception of admiration which helped keep my fire alight but wasn't its sole nourishing component. One and a half years have passed since Madrid and several successful visits to the cities of Berlin, Milan, London, Marseille and Vienna have been happily achieved in the company of friends, foreign mates and the close by in presence girlfriend.

Stockholm city with its infamous beautiful metro system and location of promising tales surrounding the topics of cross Europe Metro painters was pointed out on the map of targets and goals. Cheap flights had come into existence, but this destination was only available from the reasonable in distance airport of Milan. A friend and I reserved a fair part of a week for this occasion and in the embers of autumn we boarded the Irish plane destined for the high north. On beforehand people had told us that items and products of basic life in general up there in the northern countries overrise the prices we could already barely afford. Writers had told us not to worry, security surveillance in shops was lax so help yourself guys to whatever you might require. We weren't really grand thieves but as their actions sounded so light footed, we considered accumulating some necessities for the upcoming winter in Switzerland. Having touched the Scandinavian runway, we descended the plane and walked by foot to the small terminal building cast out in the middle of fur-tree forests miles away from Stockholm itself. A coach operating as a single shuttle service offered its pricey transfer to us after being stopped at the customs where an officer ordered his dog to sniff all over us in a side room of the entry hall, possibly indicated by my hideous dig in the nostrils as we entered the hall and our eyes had met while he overlooked the arrivals.

Once in town we waited outside the main train station for our host to pick us up. I had received the contact from a friend and had fixed the meeting earlier on. Some time passed with me and my mate cheerfully discussing our momentary observations. Coming along the pavement from around the square two guys appear and while they advance, I inspected them trying to discover clues that associated them with Graffiti. They obviously did the same. Yes, that's us we replied after we had registered each other before being certain to open our mouths. After our introduction we got into their car, good to have for painting actions, where we exchanged more information concerning our common hobby while we drove to the apartment which we were allowed to use occupied by one of the lads. They on return introduced us briefly to their life situation and what we could roughly expect to happen already from now on.

The program set for tonight sounded very encouraging and consisted a visit to a private home party, we both gleefully looked forward to that, following a visit to a commuter train yard and a go at the Metro in the early morning when service restarted. On our way to the apartment we quickly stopped next to a Metro yard, so the guys could secure some knowledge for their ongoing observation. We thought the action was already starting and they had forgotten that we didn't possess any cans yet. Hanging out by ourselves later on in the warm and cosy apartment waiting for the lads to return from family affairs and pick us up for the evening mine and Marks discussions circled the various stories of self-entitlement over products and the reputation Swedish girls had of being fairly interested in foreigners, the brown skinned dark hair male type we could fit into.

Entering the party held in an apartment, two girls on seeing us arose instantly to approach us with questions relating to our heritage and if we would like to join in on some drinks. Warmly astonished by this heart-full welcome we settled in on sofas and I engaged us in conversation to an easy-going atmosphere spread among the present young men and women. Those light-hearted blonde women sure set my brains going but I inwardly persuaded myself to stick to the commitment I had erected with the woman I was sharing an intimate relationship with. On top I wasn't that good a flirt and couldn't maintain a conversation forever so it was nice being able to say shortly after midnight that we had some actions to perpetrate and we bade farewell.

The action we fulfilled afterwards in a yard trapped in snow went nice and smooth. In the morning the lads brought us to the underground Metro station and they explained to us what we had to do. Out of reasons of concern they obliged themselves to non-engagement, but I was never the less determined to give it more than a try. Standing between the stations wall and platform the Metro train stood there awaiting the exact time to begin a new day's service and pick up transport with the driver arranging himself in his cabin. What my companion and I had to do now was to go to the other end of the train, dismount the illuminated station platform which is one and a half meters high, down onto the tracks and creep up from behind and paint standing between the wall and the wagon. Advancing towards the driver's cabin we could see he was distracted with himself, so we passed relieved that he didn't take notice of us. Walking straight further aware that our time was running I urged Mark to concentrate on the painting, it will go well, we have to get started I comfortingly suggested now that we were where we wanted to be. Let's hope he doesn't see us jumping down through his mirror we probably both thought with my heart jumping up against my gurgle. Once inside the over shaded dark canal I sketched the pieces letters and Mark followed behind filling up the space to colour in. Tension and nerve bubbling was all over us with me thinking why we had to do this alone? A second later Mark turns round saying he was off, he's leaving he urged and off he went. Seeing that the piece was nearly finished, and it would really be a shame just to follow and not complete it when we were already this far, I decided to get it done thinking things would go alright. Accelerating my tempo, I finished off inflated with adrenalin, hid the cans, poked an eye around the corner of the wagon and crept back up onto the deserted platform walking as cool as I could to the escalator, maybe the driver was looking, which brought me up from the depth to the stations entry hall where I hoped the lads would be waiting in the car outside the entrance. As I took those last steps on the moving escalator an intense gush of feelings rolled through me as I approached the turnstile with the entrance hall lying behind and the station warden in her booth. Morning light filled the hall through its entrance and towards its source I urged inwardly ready for hell to break loose but knowing that I'm either safe when through the entrance or busted. Coming outside the purple car is there standing by its own in a spacious carpark placed in front of a horizontal overall pale grey dawn break sky. Once inside my whole existence felt the relief of safety and accomplishment as I pressed myself into the front seat partly over whelmed by the action. Off we drove homewards to our beds all looking visibly relieved from the facial expressions in the quiet car.

After waking up and departing our sleeping bags we took a shower or even a bath and merrily decided to visit a close by shopping mall, so we could gain some required clothes. Like socks. We had in mind to help ourselves to whatever we thought we would need once we had seen what was on display considering the upcoming season at home. We imagined the outing to be a help yourself sprawl but once we handled the winter coats hanging there unattended in a passage way and had walked a couple of steps each with one, a firm grip took hold of my shoulder shoving me into a marching mode, unable to wedge round and I found myself moments later alone with a bulky security bloke in an office without a chance to escape. The police will be here in a few minutes he said me unsettled now and touched with anxiety. It sure won't be considered that bad I thought but what followed was complete agony. Sitting on a wooden bench I found myself shattered to tears in the sole discomfort of various cells questioning myself of the purpose of many of my handlings. The with-drawl of freedom let loose a state of being which took time to adjust too. In my eyes I had committed a minor offence and such punishment was sure to servile. Sitting on my bench not being able to see the day properly from behind tin shutters or gain access to my cigarettes left in my jacket locked away unretainable drove me to messing around with the attendance guard from a private security company who was close to hitting me while he patrolled me to my outdoor yard visit. He was unfavourable in granting me repossession of my cigarettes, so I dragged on ends left outside or rolled up some toilet paper to imitate a cigarette and its exercise while waiting for night time fall in my cell.

At last just before being driven off to court me and Mark rejoiced and found after several days of solitude comfort again in one another's company in the back of a prison transport van. Both of us had regained spirit and hoped for a parole into freedom. Together we were asked after being placed in a room in an underground garage to get up and follow. Coming in through a side door we entered a modern lively court room with judges in cloaks, prosecutors and our defence counsel greeting us with spectators seated behind him in a sealed off stand. Surprised but calm while standing stiff straight, it seemed the best way to behave I thought looking at Mark beside me unsure if he thought the same. Waiting there understanding not a word that was spoken everything appeared rather unreal (superficial) as we admitted guilty after our defender's explanation and were granted self-deportation due to our departure flight later on that day.

The judge slammed his stick down and called sternly for the next case. We bowed, smiled at each other in relief and were taken to two awaiting spacious Scandinavian cars which drove side by side apart of the way to a detention building where employees handed out our personal belongings in brown paper bags. Thankfully this fearful experience was reaching its end. There had been decent food dealt out by movie like wards with shattering views towards rising grey cliffs out of horse stable pens while permitted to suck in early morning fresh air from the cell building roof with inmate's semi visible behind metal plated fences standing next door making you wonder why they were in here.

Walking down that long gangway like passage shelled by wooded boards holding that referred to in rap songs bag and finally these long last moments of walking led to a windy pavement in the realms of the day. I breathed in the air looked around seeing city buildings with scares pedestrians in front and embraced gratefully my regained freedom.

Now that we were released and in repossession of our own will, joy spread over us and we laughed semi heart-full telling each other of our experiences and state of being during the past four days. Mark didn't go too much into details over his dealt feelings inside, he had had his cigarettes which comforted him, but we did share the same relief for the luck of having our court hearing on the day of our return flight to Switzerland. Unfortunately, through our imprisonment and us having the keys to our hosts apartment, was he as well entangled in our fate and therefor couldn't get into his home for the same spell of time. In the end when we met him in front of the house's door, we were sorry for him and his inconvenience meanwhile as much as we were for ourselves.

Arriving home later on in the evening to meet my mother and brother and sisters a phone call soon reached us that my father and the hospital were losing complete control over his health. Before I had left for Sweden, I was aware of his instable state and had asked him if I should remain around him, he had like certain times before insisted once again on me fulfilling my own plans.

Reaching the hospital with my mother a couple of hours later after my return and finding him in a desperate condition deprived of his speech hit me hard in my conscious. His tumour had spread to his brain reducing his chance of surviving his lymph cancer. Back in the car after being told that there was nothing one could do for him; I told my mother while we drove home of the occurrences that had happened to me in Sweden. On entering our apartment, the message of his death had arrived, and my existence crumbled instantly to smithereens.

How much had I loved him but had been absent a great time of the previous past, occupied with sheer self-interest and therefor missed many an occasion with him and the family. The situation dawned on me as I being too egoistic and suddenly, I began to realise what kind of an isolation I had created for myself. My focus was mainly set on my time off work with the engagements hardly shareable with anyone except my participating mates because I feared being told off or abolished from the apprentice as for being reported to the police. The closest people to me, my family didn't know what I was up too and the other way around I didn't know of their adventures. The loss of meaningful life began to expand in my perception and I came to the conclusion of giving up my graffiti actions and providing more company to the family and comforting the thoughts of my mother. Had I not made her worry a lot I thought determined to linger that effect that resulted from my actions. Amidst these sad times a short while after the funeral reasons for my cease gained more support. Totally out of the blue an investigation team from police came knocking early in the morning on the door releasing additional stress and worries. During the following months, it was autumn and up till Christmas I remained close to my family, myself and my development at work. Things that seemed important to me. Life had to go on, so I dealt with the situation and clarified my future willing to concede this phase.

A couple of days after Christmas a friend inquired if I could imagine making a small trip with him during the days off once again to Milan, our nearest Metro system, for some Metro action. At first scepticism had possession of me as I remembered my consideration to quit Graffiti altogether but being aware of the positive side to the adventure, I agreed in joining him. My main intention was to grant myself some goodness something I enjoyed and a lovely trip it was, painting in the early morning under a reddish sky after a night of snowfall outside the Metro's hangar during half an hour time while the lads who were taking some driving lessons with the composition went for their tee break. Extremely happy with our achievement and aware of my fondness towards the whole activity and adventure I allowed myself to reengage with the painting and its scene but not to a stage of overdoing my dedication and I would share my activity slightly broader from now on, it was my pleasure and nothing to be ashamed of.

Thinking of what it would mean to quit totally around now got me to recognise the fact that I would miss out on meddling with the city of Graffiti's birth. That occurred to me as kind of ungrateful towards the creators of my ongoing culture and I surly would close the circle one day by giving back what I had developed through personified acclaimation. New York City and it's Metro system had always been a stunning magnet to me, even more when equivalents devotionally shared their story of action otherwise it was hard to miss if you used a television. Graffiti never seemed to fully cease in its Metro format in the City and the New York Evening Herald brandished Europeans as the ill cause of it, calling it and them in their papers headline, trash.

New York City

In the ongoing year our semi-orphan accomplished successfully his apprenticeship and was happy and eager to experience his independence won through age and the fact he could deal with his earnings as he pleased so-far he had an occupation that provided any.

The note of liberty scheduled his work efforts to an impact that provided enough time off and earnings to meet the states expected payments and his modest involvement's in life which didn't change particularly to what he had been doing until now.

Years pasted by with sporadic escapades erupting through the blend of life and strong booze resulting in self-assessment and reflection. Thanks to a befriended semi Englishmen in his football team who kindly made him aware of the aptitude he thought he had for entertainment, because he mostly messed around verbally trying to make a surplus to the humour going on in the dressing room. Knock a bit of the craic one would say in Ireland. Taking his advice serious he looked around for opportunities to channel his energies into and on discovering small theatre clubs he got himself involved.

Circling around his world nearly at the same time painting friends who slowly but definitely were giving up their enthusiasm for the Graffiti engagement had ventured into Latin America and were now telling inviting tales of the time spent over there. Naturally his curiosity was activated, and he was happy to be asked to join those lads on their next trip to South America. To make such trips possible meant for him that austerity would have to rain his personal household for a couple of months. His cooking wage at the time paid by an indexed company was more or less poor for general Swiss income and it was all in all a though challenge to get the required 4 and a half grand together in half a year. The amount was considered just about enough for three months. Aside the ticking of the calendar box bore to him the note of advancement towards the trip.

Once enough money was saved for the flight could planning begin. And what an idea came up. We would fly via New York City instead of via a European city to reach our Latin American destination.

At last the encounter with the city and his prolonged wish for painting there could find an approach. Eager for the painting adventure the main stop in New York was planned for the return journey from Latin America to Europe in case of inconveniences that could erupt through painting and block the outbound flight.

Arriving after a two-day stopover in New York the four lads touched down on Colombian tarmac and were greeted on the threshold of the plane by striking tropical heat. Three months were lying ahead of the group for travel and excursion. Two months got spent across Colombia with the month in between occupied with a round tour of Central America by public transport.

Thinking themselves fortunate for being able to return to Europe (Switzerland) where everything is organised and developed the home journey got cheerfully attended with the lengthier stopover in New York half way.

Unfortunately, when painting the NYC Subway with one out of the quartet, he thought his piece was on its way to become a burner but suddenly the lights in the Subway sprang into function putting the question of a safe retreat towards the two of them. Which they considered wise and afterwards did.

Back in Switzerland our young man in his early twenties was slightly disappointed in not having achieved his painting goal but on the other hand felt bemused knowing a return at a later point in life was inevitable.

The waters temperature is turned well towards boiling point and I'm sitting on the floor of the shower cabin cuddled up with my legs pulled close up to my chest dozing in and out of sleep underneath the hot jets of water descending upon me. This is my way of showering when I need some extra comfort.

I'm up late alright but confident that I'll reach the airports gate in time.

A couple of hours ago I was enjoying the company of two females and we danced together enhanced by a couple of glasses of Cuba Libré to matching tunes till the mornings early hours, me celebrating my soon departure to New York two years after my last visit and the women a midweek opportunity to gay (jovial) life.

Once showered into the right mood and dressed casually I set out to the Airport on an efficient route to ensure my punctual arrival. A painting comrade of mine has arranged a meeting for us with an old friend of his who is living at home in Brooklyn New York. When he told me of his intentions, I smelt instantly a perfect opportunity for my lingering prime goal. The central fact that made the opportunity perfect was more the reason that we would be able to share the space and time of New Yorker's.

By now it meant a lot to me being able to accompany local people in their home town structures. It gave every visit and journey a profound experience which I certainly wished and tried to arrange for myself when away from home.

The mate I'm going to share the visit with is also an eager chap and a good few years older than myself and I believe it to be fortunate that we have at least one goal in common.

Our flights arrive in New Jersey and we take a public bus towards a further station taking us on into the City of New York. Looking out the bus window in mid-afternoon New Jersey ain't looking very prosperous I think to myself as we pass by a gloomy dark brown bricked environment showing signs of neglect and over infrastructural protection. Till we reach Brooklyn we're sharing the company of city commuters and I'm enjoying curiously my observation for signs of difference between us Europeans and them Yankees. The utilisation of the subway appears to function just the same as in Europe except that they have additional express lines beside the persisting one and it's not that easy to get in without a ticket. I'm happy to see the shine of the subway but more positively anxious about who we are going to meet and what's going to go down in the coming ten days of my visit. The sound of the American accent arising over standing and sitting heads is awesome, I'm listening closely warming up my own inner Yank ready to let him out as soon as an opportunity arises.

Disembarking the subway close to the end of one of the Brooklyn lines we emerge out of the station inhaling icy air which loosens shivers as we walk up the stairs onto the pavement of a long borough high street. The street is side parked with vehicles and flanked by shops in two story brick-built buildings. In search of our contact a small man tucked in thick winter clothes smiling through a mouth rimed with a beard calls for our attention as we look around in search of him. He is accompanied by his smiling wife who has the typical appearance of the warm and friendly Latin American in her soft and wide round red cheeked face. My mate full of joy embraces him and her heartfully and after some vocal courtesy I get the chance to introduce myself. We should be off and they've been grocery shopping they say as we walk towards their loft accommodation, them pulling the typical New Yorker hand cart beholding their purchases.

Looking up towards the roofs of the flat buildings a thin sheet of snow can be seen upon rims, meaning that the harsh icy wind blowing around us is sustaining winter's season in the end phase of the month January. Our hosts inform us before we enter their spacious ground floor loft that there heating is missing the required energy, so we hopefully have got enough suitable clothes with us to keep ourselves warm especially when in bed at night. I wouldn't consider packing carelessly in this time of season and to keep comfort have brought the whole gear with me. Sleeping bag, long johns, woolly socks, gloves, hat plus track suit trousers for the home time. I'm not a fan of having to tolerate low temperatures. Once we've passed the entrance the extent of the space is can be seen. It is one big room designed originally for a repair shop of motorized vehicles and by what one sees the couple have creatively redefined the available space. Upon wooden stilts stand sealed carpeted wooden boxes or cubes with a window and curtain to it which offer themselves as individual rooms and one is for me and my companion. A previous office room is now Hectors creative (atelier) hub where he keeps his utensils for his Artworks. He does paintings. On the other side of the main room built up against the wall stands confirm and general looking a kitchen structure with a dining table placed in front and its accompanying chairs around it. Beneath one of the high posted boxes integrated in a separated cabin below is the refreshment room beholding everything a westerner would require for his or her body rituals including a small electrical heating fit for contemplation. Placed on the walls vacant space just below the tin-plated roof are the room's windows as well as set in some parts of the roof. All in all, an impressive solution for a space to be converted into dwelling created by this sympatric couple. We talked and got to know each other while the couple prepared a meal with us two lending a hand when required. Through the turns in our conversations I was able to estimate a slight disapproval for certain practises and entanglements embedded in American capitalism and felt relieved in finding a common knowledge between us which we shared. They both had immigrated to New York from Latin America which allowed them a distinct perception and point of view. Their homelands had and still have bonds to the dominant northern whipper. During the night tucked tightly in my sleeping bag pulled up over my face and covered with additional blankets the coldness still woke me now and then nagging away especially at my feet. All I had as an answer was too curl up even tighter. The following two days my companion and me visited Manhattan on his insistence and towards the dusk of the day met up with the couple who in the meantime had attended to their duties. They took us on walks through the borough a long its high streets and into its belonging Sunset Park where one had a wonderful view out over the water onto Manhattan with its sky scrapping shining mirror buildings. Around us in the park on the slight descending ridges children sledged happily on a firm bed of snow and my mate touched by what he saw supplemented the moment by playing on his mobile phone Alicia Key's song of New York City. His action seemed a bit kitsch, but it fulfilled it's purpose in releasing positive thoughts accompanied by laughter and cuddles. You could also acknowledge it as our interlude because tonight was also going to be our first painting attempt on the Subway. Thoughts where already arising twitching every now and then a nerve in my body which summoned knots in my stomach. After a late dinner at home on our base we prepared our utensils professionally and listened concentrated to what our host had to say about our declared location for the action. Our approach on the target was set for after dinner telly time and as the borough showed signs of village life the Subway station was sure going to be quiet in this period of the night meaning it was bound to be deserted. Though not to be forgotten were the slow patrolling cop cars on the streets which weren't rare at any time of the day.

Adapting to the minus temperatures outside, we dressed warm and set out on our underground mission. Once inside the station we boarded an operating Subway to pass our parked Subway which lay behind the station between two functioning lines. Many Subway compositions were coupled together and extended the one we had in mind painting, filling up the whole length of the tunnel between two stations. As we passed the parked colons of steel, we spied the best we could through our carriages window for lights and movements amidst the territory we were about to set foot on. Nothing suspicious was made out so our intrusion was going to take place as soon as the Subway in service had left the station. No security surveillance was installed anywhere so we just had to wait till the disembarking passengers had exited the station. The last was out of sight and off we went towards the end of the platform down the steps pushing aside the small "Precaution danger" shield and into the tunnels dimly lit space we walked. As we approached the parked subways standing in overall silence a slightly warmer air greeted us from their pillared in position. This wasn't exactly the sight we wanted to see them in but never the less we were here now and there was three meters of space for painting between each pillar.

The model although squared in, delighted me because of its vintage feel to the steel channels running along its side which I always had wanted for a surface and asserting myself we might see it in traffic the following morning which I assumed would mean being lucky.

Listening for a couple of moments for anything to be heard I looked at my companion and he indicated for me to start painting. All seems to be in a safe condition, so I began. We have over ten minutes over ten minutes to finish our pieces and get out of the tunnel. I'm painting in a steady pace adjusted to the time available when suddenly, I'm doing my outlines, my man next to me comes over and tells me to hurry up because he's going in a second. Me flabbergasted by his request respond that we still have time and I have more letters to fulfil than he has. Inside I'm boiling, feeling affronted by his lack of loyalty and sense for the whole occasion. We're in the tunnel together and if he leaves without me I'm exposed to a greater risk due to his single reverse onto the platform which could withhold people with loose lips. A second later he turns and is gone. I'm disgustedly angry but never the less this piece is going to get finished. Three steps on my piece have to get completed and I do them under a spell of firm driven speed and after four minutes I finish off with the outlines. Once outside the station I meet up with him and confront him, but nothing is really to help. What has happened lies behind us and he hasn't got much to say for himself follow-ing my declaration of how things should be taken care of. My angriness wears off and I'm feeling content and happi-ly bemused with myself for remaining and succeeding to accomplish my first New York City Subway. On our way home, we agree to buy some snacks, so we enter one of the many night shops selling groceries, candy and loads of booze. Seeing my companion reach out for a bottle of coke which I there upon suggest is a bad idea referring to the topics our hostess had previously talked about but I also don't want to accelerate into a discussion now. The next morning as we awoke and entered the kitchen space, writ-ten upon the sugar and fizz left on the table, read one of the side effects it withholds. It kills Unions. True enough I think resuming the landscapes of Guatemala with their vast sugar cane plantations and I had thought she wouldn't be impressed having to host that shit.

A day later while we were at our breakfast her hus-band and my companion who had in the meantime had some discussions, in Spanish, where now obviously reveal-ing to me that we had to leave their home. My companion mentioned the discomforting situation released by the heating disabilities continuing that it would be better we sought a dwelling somewhere else. The "we" wasn't in-cluded in the new dwelling option because his other friend who lived in town and offered to host him wouldn't be able to provide an additional space for me. The new situation didn't concern me, more the opposite evolved out of the upcoming challenge. The sense of independent decision making illuminated my outlook for the remaining week and we agreed to keep in touch and meet up with one an-other. This separation meant a new episode of my stay was about to begin and I had the single power of its direc-tion. Thinking of my new dwelling I hoped I could organise a place in the too me familiar hostel from my earlier visit up in east Haarlem where I liked the surroundings. Central Park lay a couple of blocks away with the neighbourhood in between consisting of brown brick high rises aside five to six story buildings with shops in its bottom added by grocery stores, corner shops, laundry parlours and numerous deli grocers from all nations of the world. Some of the buildings walls in that area were decorated with murals displaying a relation to Hispanic bio-tops (culture). Loud music could be heard blaring out of shops or from speakers set beside street stalls and the out of the slow driving cars with the shiny rims carrying the cool stunt'n human inside. Being able to return to this place meant I could adapt and participate to a slight degree with ongoing life and acknowledge a deeper domestic feeling. This hood displayed a glimpse of genuine New York life which I gladly embraced seeing that it extended my main interests of discovering and experiencing New York. After my inquiries over the internet the hostel had accommodation on offer for me and I bade farewell to the two men and I set out to begin the next episode.

In the following days I undertook long walks to various parts of the city where I bumped into the Chinese New Year procession with a colourful long tailed dragon gliding over the heads of the people carrying it on long sticks or passed through a Jewish neighbourhood with their orthodox dressed inhabitants going about their duties. Further I ventured into parts of the town I had picked its name up previously in life and had remembered again such as Bushwick or looked out for places on the map with interesting names. Knickerbocker Avenue sounded curious, so I arrived there to exiting a tattered and leaking run-down Subway station and walked down its avenue or more so high street to discover that there existed neglected and poorly maintained infrastructure in city. Otherwise I didn't come across anything stunning. Places of interest where also streets and areas such as the meat packing district or Broadway, places I had read about in Irish novels and went out searching for any remaining traces and descriptions from the twenties, but nothing really was to be found that I had in mind. Manhattan had obviously mutated and resettled itself because the only remaining relics where a couple of Irish pubs withholding never the less a descendant but not the feverish impoverished drink pursuers from the 20th centuries beginning. So, deprived of company I stemmed my glass in solitude toasting to man's and woman's family fortune in those harsh days. A night on I met up with my friend and his friends took us out to a funk party which truly withheld the spirit of the golden eighties as the visitors who filled the club up to its every corner swayed in harmony to the musical pearls played aloud. The atmosphere inside left us impressed and we danced and smiled all happy and good spirited as one could be toasting with the juice. This state of being enhanced by my holistic experiences here in town led me to close and warm dancing with wonderful lip and mouth counter pressing with a blonde enthusiastic city girl who cuddled in dance which I due to the distance of the home travel rejected from deeper physical involvement. When the time arrived for our departure and we bunch of men mounted the stairs back up to the street the blizzard that had been announced to hit New York had arrived. Upon everything lay a fresh cover of half a meter snow and the only vehicles moving on the streets were snow plough trucks with their orange circling flashlights. Quietness and peace lay in the air as we walked knee deep through the light snow each ploughing a path merrily from crossroad to crossroad under the falling snow flakes also regaining the streets full space while snowball throwing engaging passer-by's. The next day as I had breakfast by myself again, I had the city's Herald beside me for a journalistic insight and I came across the information that many Subways would get relocated to the tunnels from their outdoor depots for the reason of protection from the intense cold weather. Straight away my mind took up the abandon tunnel and station me and a friend had discovered and explored on the earlier stopover in the city and I was nearly definite that this would be my chance to complete an action on the Subway in the fashion I wished and imagined an action to progress.

An unexpected meeting
The tunnel I had previously come across passed through the Old Italian quarters in lower Manhattan and descended out onto the Williamsburg Bridge. As we were out walking about that area of the island, we grew weary and decided to grant our legs a break. The neighbourhood hadn't shown anything particular Italian but the place had the brick buildings with the typical fire escapes going along the outside of their shell. The narrow streets passing below gave the place a sense of an old town compared to other parts of lower Manhattan and it was scarcely (densely) animated. Looking around for a Subway station we found one a block or two around a corner and entered it thinking of being moved on. Inside no one was to be seen and it was unattended and in a derelict state. Set along in a strip above the tracks under the ceiling between the white tiles were still visible nice mosaic decorations. While we were standing on the platform looking around and waiting for the ride to arrive I realised that the white tiled wall beyond the tracks had small arches set in it and bending down to look through one I could clearly see another platform. As seeing a platform, it struck me more to see tags placed on

the tiles beyond which was rather unusual for NYC Subway stations. I told my mate and we came to the conclusion that it was probably a closed part of the station and worthwhile exploring. Down off the platform we jumped and crossed over to find as we thought an abandon station covered in numerous tags but none that we recognised. Content with our discovery we walked on the tracks into the tunnel to sense the atmosphere with the operating Subways passing by. This is something I've always enjoyed doing and mainly favoured painting in such depths of the city. I got to like leaving the common town surface and disappear into underground roads and spaces which belonged to the city, but you never would think of gaining access to. In general, it had a sticky smell and it was slightly warmer than outside and a silent peacefulness hovered through its dim lit long stretched tubes winding off round a bend into the unknown. The only thing sometimes to be heard was a dull stud or rattle from canalization lids being pressed down by-passing cars above. One was alone, vanished from the earth's surface and free to walk and tag and do pieces as one wished for a certain time before climbing up a metal ladder attached to the tunnels wall or located in a room behind a door in the walls leading back to the cosmos dominated by humans.

If I'm lucky the MTA will store a composition or two down here, so the electrified joints of the carriages will be out of nature's icy spell.

I've got myself a decent colour setting put together and I'm off just after midnight on my own curious but maintaining the possibility of being disappointed towards my full comprehensive opportunity. An urge inside me is towing me towards the spot withholding my long-declared goal and I determinedly obey my wish. My dwelling is safe and I'm secure that I'm prepared and agitate to succeed alone. The vandal squad can gladly stay away but if anything arises I'm ready and passionate to sustain my ground and liberty. Sitting in the Subway, cans placed between my legs on the floor tucked in a Swiss string handle backpack I hope I appear to be a labourer on his way home and nod off every now and then dropping my kin onto my chest.

Some among us small number of passengers are sleeping properly slumped to one side or leaning the head downwards like I'm doing. Arriving at my destination I remain inside the carriage waiting to take a discreet glance through the window while passing the spot of hope on the way to the following station. What do I see as I look down at the small arches in the tiled wall...yes, the pale surface of grey steel confronts my eyes. Moving into the tunnel my heart and spirit are jumping as more of my good fortune shines into light as the traveling Subway casts its headlights on parts of the parked Subway now standing next to us in the dark. Having passed the inhabited (occupied) spot I'm now growing lightly nervous confronted with the existence of my searched reality which can now be realised. Everything looked superficially calm. I've disembarked and re-embarked at the following station. Passing by again I can make out weak lights set in the wall behind the parked Subway which is crucially important. It would be a nonsense to paint in total darkness, you can't see what you're doing which would be pitiful. Before I advance to my final exit, I consider how I'm going to undertake my approach and execution. Just before the Subway comes to a halt, I notice looking sideways through the windows in the rear of my carriage two young men standing in the next carriage in front of the doors like me.

Straight away I realise that I might not be the only writer possessing the idea of painting here. Not to worry I think, and I exit the carriage quick and inconspicuously, too hide behind the elevator shaft. Curious I observe from the unseen what these guys must have in mind because dangling in their hands are plastic bags contending six pack boxes for spray cans. I wait observing them through the glass walls of the elevator shaft for the Subway to disappear out of the station and to make sure no other people stay behind in the station. Aware that no one else is here except us a little friendly meant joke crosses my mind. I'll make the scene appear to be touched by an air of normality and I emerge out my hiding place advancing towards the two dauntless men. Both are wearing baseball caps and dressed in understatement except for the blonde man who is keeping himself warm with a modern hunting coat illustrated with sticks and branches. The men look the same age as me and are discussing as I approach unnoticed from behind. Hey guys, you off for some action as well I ask them as I stand next to them pointing at their bags grinning broadly. Agreeing with my question I purpose for us to clear the platform and enter the tunnel. The two tell me while we move forward that they knew of the options resolving out of harsh winter weather and were curious like me to see if the circumstances matched our beliefs.

Once behind the tiled wall dividing the station into the old and new part, we stood still then crouched down to listen for any noises emerging out of the silence. Nothing was to be heard so we agreed after introducing ourselves properly to one another to make out a good painting spot in the cave of the tunnel because although the Subway was standing right in front us and well illuminated, we could get spotted much easier. At first for a short moment I was puzzled thinking that these two guys could be bait for a trap. But this occurred to me to be too absurd, so I happily rejoiced to have come across company. On we moved into the darkness crossing the border of decorated to neglected tunnel and walked (sideways) along the Subway train composition. A couple of moments later we entered a space opening up into the tunnels full wideness with numerous tracks gliding off out of our weakly lit position into further darkness. Looking around in the weak light we could make out two carriages standing in a curve. Seeing that a straight view along the compositions was there for broke suited us wonderfully adding to the superb concrete floor under our feet. Calmness spread out among us as we waited in a covered spot for the Subway trains in service to pass by. Everything in this layup occurred to be as it favourably should be, quiet and unattended. The Subways rattled passed us casting an enormous portion of light for several seconds on our object of desire and as it rolled out of ear shot we got into position holding our cans in place ready to start. Onto my toes I stretched myself drawing my sketch beneath the trenched in blood American flag. I was keen to have it visible on the surface of my piece to underline the interaction on their imperialistic mainland. A self-inflict like the placement of a foreign flag on hostile ground or the flagpole sticking in the soil of an alien planet. Enjoying the ongoing situation and realising that at last I was doing the original of the close to me culture, friendly accompanied by two likewise minded humans made me happy and comfortable. This was it colour sticking to a surface of impact changing its monotone appearance plus my eager and passionate developed motion was resembled in a form of letters representing my existence. Whilst engaged with drawing the last of my lines I suddenly had to realise when standing back and overlooking content my piece for a moment that shamefully once again I had mismanaged my painting space and come to close to the other fellow's production. Seeing that he was well advanced it was simply too late for corrections I thought thinking meanwhile of hitting up the face and nose of the Subway train with tags for more expression to the adventure. This meant the inner strain calling weakly for a safe retreat would have to chill and secure confidence which it did while we climbed around on the front of the Subway placing our names and catching the moments. Disturbing the quietness an engine cracked into action crabbing our attention by the instant. Easy I signalled, this happened regularly knowing the Subway trains weren't disconnected totally from the power channels and sometimes they sprung into some sort of operation for a couple of minutes. As the noise continued we listened carefully aware that it could also mean human activity and from somewhere around us in the tunnel the crackling of Walkie Talkies frequencies pierced the mechanical noise clearly to be heard. Agreeing that we all heard the additional noise our definite conclusion was that maintenance workers were on the approach with the intention of getting the composition ready for the day's journey although we weren't sure what time it was.

Hastily we collected our bags of paint to store them in a place out of sight before exiting the tunnel onto the operated platform. The station was empty. Considering that the MTA workers were preparing the roll out which had to be in the direction of Williamsburg we agreed to take the next Subway to the following station for an overview of our work.

Arriving on the other side of the bridge we became aware that the roll out wouldn't happen straight away because it was only yet three o'clock in the morning and rush hour wouldn't start before six o'clock. Hunger made its appearance within us and we went to a corner store situated below the elevated tracks that our pieces were going to pass upon for some cheese, ham, eggs on a roll and hot please. Undertaking this would also mean we could win an overview of what was going on outside the station. You thought the vandal squad might have caught wind of our work and decided to copy us for an effective impression and encounter. After eating the tasty hot sandwich and a half an hour of waiting finally our subway train had its turn to leave its sleeping place and it glided passed us upon the thick layer of snow in front of the nights background. It was a quick display, a blink of an eye and with a long look following its quick appearance but none the less that's what you get and it made me and the other two happy being able to see it running the city.

The three of us standing there on the long-stretched platform in the freezing cold seeing that the mission was over were happy and totally content with the outcome of the evening. We remained a while in each other's company exchanging more of our backgrounds giving each other an insight of the Graff scenes we participated with.

Biding one another farewell we separated, and I returned to my hostel in the left overs of the night in a still sleeping city covered by the spell of bitter coldness.

The end of my stay is nearly reached, and I spent the last of the days visiting museums wondered along Broadway in search of something interesting and made a visit to Jersey Gardens for the advantage of low-price clothing items but on examining the garments I noticed that most of the stuff lacked a genuine quality and shape.

When night time arrived, I still had some cans left over, the urge to paint arouse and overcame me with me unable to abandon the thought of doing so. Shouldn't I paint as much as I could? "I'm here in New York and should do as much as I can," where some of my insisting thoughts opposite the fact of being safe and having fulfilled my wish. Knowing that a spot for a third attempt lay close by my hostel persuaded me to try some more but some-how, I entered the tunnel from the wrong side of the plat-form and ended up enjoying a stroll in the concrete canals with a later hastily light-footed escape into a safety dent in the wall initiated by an oncoming Subway. Well it obvious-ly didn't want to happen so I gave up any further efforts and controlled myself to be satisfied with what I had achieved.

This was it "the big city of dreams" entangled with one of mine and me now proud of myself for having succeeded in reaching a goal and in achieving a contribution to New York Graffiti in the year 2011. Standing on top of my high-rise dwelling, set around me building after building with millions of windows and beyond them the east river flow-ing grey and restless into the Atlantic sea. Life was good I felt alive engaging with our cosmoses meaning no harm, had overcome the loss of my father's inexistence, separat-ed myself from the dear woman at one time for the sake of living diversity, felt warmth and love for much and was happy being able to explore and discover. Wondering to-day five years later with my out-inward gaze from that mo-ment while leaning on the railing, is this the epi centre of modern western culture, Americanisation to some degree I think to myself regarding to Europe's tendency of by-cul-tural hegemony (charity). Considering how New York's aspect is present on many scales, omnipresent on many surfaces and looming as a cultural phenomenon.

Below my rooftop place across the wide road filled with traffic in between a line of brown brick high rises kids are playing basketball on a court till suddenly one of the kids jumps into Hip Hop dancing steps and instantly every-one on the court joins in to perform a stunning chorogra-phy of unified movement.